ONE MAN'S MEAT

The Lincolnshire town of Flaxborough seems respectable enough, with many professionals living there, but young Robert Digby Tring's sudden death in the fairground again brings a shock to the inhabitants.

Julia Harton is married to a rising pet food executive but becomes involved in 'Happy Endings Inc'—what exactly is this organisation?

Inspector Purbright must delve deep to find the truth about the town's mysteries . . .

ONE MAN'S MEAT

Colin Watson

First published 1977
by
Eyre Methuen

This edition 2004 by BBC Audiobooks Ltd
published by arrangement with
the author's estate

ISBN 1 4056 8505 0

British Library Cataloguing in Publication Data available

Printed and bound in Great Britain by
Antony Rowe Ltd., Chippenham, Wiltshire

A WORD FROM YOUR AUTHOR

It was necessary to the plot of this book to invent the names of a couple of processed dog foods and to ascribe to their supposed manufacturers titles that would neither duplicate nor suggest those of any real firms. The most diligent inquiries were made. They led rapidly to two discoveries: first, that the pet food industry dwarfs in scale and complexity some of the biggest enterprises in the field of human nutrition; second, that no word in the English language (or, indeed, out of it) can safely be discounted as a potential brand name, however tenuous its canine connotations.

Having regard to the difficulties and hazards presented by this situation, and in pursuance of my aim to avoid causing moral, aesthetic, religious, patriotic or commercial distress to any one of the several thousand patentees, proprietors and distributors of foodstuffs for domestic animals, I hereby solemnly declare that all such substances and their manufacturers mentioned in this book are purely imaginary and have nothing to do with the real and beautiful world in which we live.

In particular, I affirm that the imaginary product Woof referred to in the book is in no way connected with or intended to resemble the actual product which is an expanded complete packed dog food manufactured and marketed by BP Nutrition (U.K.) Limited, under that name.

Chapter One

THE SPACE MODULE 'HERMES' SWUNG HIGH ABOVE ITS revolving mother ship. The lights of other bodies streamed past the observation window. They came and went too quickly to be identified, but companion modules were there, sharing the same orbit.

The noise, which at launching had been an ear-splitting amalgam of machinery, sirens and amplified last-minute instructions, was now much diminished. It consisted in the main of piped rock and roll music. This doubtless was to be a substantial ingredient of the cosmonauts' sustenance in space.

The craft held a crew of two. Their ponderous suits and great gourd-like helmets concealed all clues to age and sex. They sat in moulded chairs, one behind the other, facing the nose cone of the module.

One of the helmet visors was pushed up just sufficiently to allow speech. The other crewman, staring out of a port, did not at first respond. Gloved knuckles rapped against his head-globe. He turned and raised his vent.

The cosmonauts conversed. Their gestures were lively, but not well coordinated. A terrestial observer might have supposed them slightly drunk – an effect of weightlessness, perhaps.

One struck the release buckles of his seat harness and pushed the straps impatiently aside. The other stopped talking and watched with interest, as if waiting for his companion to float around the cabin. Nothing happened, so he, too, freed himself.

Both appeared to be a good deal elated by their emancipation. One unstoppered a space-flask and sucked at the stimulant within, then held the flask out, offering it. The other removed his helmet and placed it between his knees. He took the flask.

Drinking from it greedily, he made heroic gestures with his free arm.

A string of bright orange moons moved across the blackness framed in the observation window. The crew member who held the flask stared at them in surprise. Suddenly he was on the floor of the module. The vehicle had lurched.

There was some scrambling, boisterous but apparently good-natured. Helmet and space-flask left the floor and began to roll up the bulkhead and across the roof. So did the cosmonaut from whose grip they had escaped.

The module had entered that part of its programme which required it to revolve about its own axis, in accordance with the principle whereby space travellers are provided with a simulation of homely gravity.

Unhappily for the cosmonaut who had abandoned his seat harness (the other had never altogether relinquished hold upon his safeguard and was now securely strapped once more) there became operative at that moment what space agencies would have termed an extra-programmatic circumstance.

The vehicle's ingress-egress hatch – its door, one might almost say – opened and swung outward.

Towards the black rectangle thus revealed trundled the flask as the module continued to turn. It hung at the rim for a moment, obstructed by a shallow flange, then suddenly disappeared into space.

The unharnessed cosmonaut was too preoccupied with trying to regain control over his own movement to notice the flask's departure. If he had, he might have had time to reason out the precursive significance of the event and see his danger.

By the time the module's revolution had brought him to the brink of the open hatchway, the cosmonaut was in that state of relaxation which frequently succeeds, if only momentarily, a period of playful physical exuberance.

He tumbled out in a flopping somersault without a cry; not into orbit, but in shallow parabola towards the gravitational centre of the planet earth, the nearest to which he got was the pavement outside the shop of Mr James Arliss, gentlemen's outfitter and bespoke tailor, in Market Place, Flaxborough.

Chapter Two

INQUESTS, DECLARED MR HARCOURT CHUBB, MBE, Chief Constable of Flaxborough, were not much in his line, so it was Detective Inspector Purbright who attended the inquiry into the 'Hermes' accident.

He addressed the coroner, a red-faced, punctilious young solicitor named Cannon, who had taken the job over twelve months before on the almost indetectable transition of the previous office-holder, Sir Albert Amblesby, from a comatose to a clinically lifeless condition.

'This case arises from an accident in Flaxborough Fair on Saturday night, sir,' said the inspector. 'The fair is held, as you will know, in an area of the Market Place between West Row and the Corn Exchange, and it includes a number of mechanical rides.'

Mr Cannon nodded sapiently. He had a big note pad in front of him, as well as a pile of ready-typed depositions by witnesses.

'One of the rides was called Space Shot,' said the inspector.

'Space Shot?' echoed the coroner, affecting dubiousness.

'Yes, sir. The owner of the ride will be able to give you details if you require them, but I gather that the idea is to provide its passengers with a feeling of flight through space. They occupy a series of cars – or modules, is that right?' – Purbright glanced aside inquiringly at a large, whiskered man in a green velveteen suit, who said yes, that indeed was correct – 'each of which holds two people. The passengers are provided with seat belts and there are prominent notices urging their use.

'An attendant has instructions – or so we understand – to see that riders have fastened their belts before the machine starts. He also is supposed to check the bolts securing the car doors. These can be operated from either inside or outside the modules, and are pretty substantial, as one would expect.'

There was movement at the back of the room. 'That bloody thing wasn't safe!' A woman in a sky-blue hat, face taut with anger and grief, was being held back in her chair by shushing neighbours. 'There's a boy dead 'cos o' that.'

Mr Cannon scowled and seemed about to issue an interdict. There looked up at his left shoulder the gentle moon-face of Sergeant William Malley, Coroner's Officer, with whispered counsel.

'The boy's auntie, sir. Very cut up.'

Mr Cannon turned his attention to the inspector once more.

'Shortly before midnight on Saturday,' Purbright resumed, 'an ambulance was called to the Market Place, where a young man was lying injured – possibly already dead – having fallen from the fair ride I have been describing. He was identified as Robert Digby Tring, aged 23, a pet-food processing technician – is that right, sergeant?'

'That's how the job's described, sir.'

'Thank you. And he lived with other members of the family, including his grandmother, at 18 Abdication Avenue. He wasn't married, I gather – or was he?'

'No, sir. Not married. You're probably confusing him with Joseph.'

Purbright said 'Ah', looked in silence at his notes for a moment or two, then asked the coroner if he would like the first witness called.

Mr Cannon was not sure that he cared for the tradition of informality at Flaxborough inquests that allowed the sort of side conversation between Purbright and Malley into which they had just drifted. But nor was he confident of his ability to manage affairs on his own. These local people were unpredictable; they could be truculent. Moreover there was someone present in court on that particular occasion of whom the coroner stood in too much awe to risk throwing his weight about.

'Very well, inspector,' said Mr Cannon.

There came to the table over which the coroner presided a man of about 30 with black hair and deep sideburns, a mahogany complexion and a loping, careless walk.

Purbright invited him to the chair which Malley had drawn out for him.

'Your name is Patrick Harold Tring?' inquired the coroner, glancing up from the deposition he had taken from the top of the pile.

'Aye.'

'You are aged 32 years, a storekeeper, and you reside at 18 Abdication Avenue, Flaxborough?'

'Aye.'

'And you identify the body you were shown last Sunday morning in the mortuary of Flaxborough General Hospital as that of your brother, Robert Digby Tring?'

'Digger. Aye. It was.'

'How old was he, Mr Tring?'

Tring indicated Purbright with his head. 'Like the policeman said. Twenty-three.'

'And he resided with you and the other members of the family?'

'Aye. We all sort of muck in together like. With Gran. I already told him.' This time it was Sergeant Malley at whom Tring nodded.

'Yes, well, I have to hear it from your own lips, Mr Tring,' the coroner explained. He paused. 'By Gran, I presume you mean your grandmother, do you?'

The possibility that there might be anyone in Flaxborough unacquainted with the redoubtable Grandma Tring struck the witness as so bizarre that for several seconds he could only stare at Mr Cannon. Then he looked down the room at the knot of people whence the earlier interjection had come and grinned clannishly.

'Well, I don't mean my soddin' uncle, do I?'

This earned squawks of commendation from kin and the very acidly expressed news from Mr Cannon that Mr Tring was in a courtroom and not upon the stage of a music hall.

'Your brother was not married?'

'No.'

'So far as you know, he was in good health?'

There was nothing, averred Mr Tring, the matter with Digger.

'That is all I have to ask you,' said the coroner, 'but these other gentlemen may wish to put questions to you.' He indicated Purbright and, further off, a sleek, silvery-grey man whose very presence looked as if it was going to cost somebody a lot of money even if he made no further contribution to the proceedings.

The inspector said there was nothing else the police wished to ask this witness. Mr Cannon turned to the silver-grey man and offered him a deferential smile.

Mr Raymond Plant-Huntleigh, Q.C., accepted the smile and sent a much more splendid one back. He rose with athletic grace.

'You appear, Mr Plant-Huntleigh, I understand, on behalf of the Fair and Pleasure Garden Proprietors' Protection Association,' said the coroner.

'That is my privilege, sir.'

'Pray proceed.'

The barrister gazed upon Mr Tring with a sort of grieved affection. 'May I express the deep sympathy of my clients and, indeed, of myself, with the family of this young man, so tragically deprived of life at a time when it must have been full of promise.'

Mr Tring rubbed his jaw. 'Yes, well . . .' He shuffled. 'That's all right. I mean, it's not your fault, is it?'

'I commend your generosity in a time of sorrow,' said Mr Plant-Huntleigh. He watched Mr Cannon's pen making its slow addenda to the typed deposition.

Purbright said something to Sergeant Malley, who squeezed nearer the coroner and murmured in his ear. Mr Cannon seemed a little annoyed, but he nodded and addressed the witness.

'Is the family legally represented?' he asked.

'D'you mean have I got a solicitor? No – well, I mean it's not as if I was up in court for something, is it?'

'You are entitled to be represented, nevertheless. However, I shall give you what guidance I can in the event of your being asked any question you might feel doubtful about.' Mr Cannon glanced at the inspector. 'All right, Mr Purbright?' Purbright made a small bow.

The barrister appeared to be in the most cordial agreement with Mr Cannon's undertaking. He beamed upon Tring and said: 'Let us revert very briefly to the matter of your brother's state of health. Nothing the matter with Digger, I believe you said. Hale and hearty young chap, was he?'

'You could say that, yeah.'

'And full of high spirits on occasion, eh?'

'Well, he was only young, wasn't he?'

'Indeed he was, alas. Indeed he was.' Mr Plant-Huntleigh guessed – rightly – that cross-examination was no novelty to Mr Tring. He took a little longer to lead up to his next question.

'You have heard, I have no doubt, the time-honoured phrase "All the fun of the fair," ' he said. 'Fairs are places for fun, for enjoyment – enjoyment, it may be, of a somewhat boisterous kind sometimes. Nothing wrong with that, of course. Now do you agree that your brother would not hesitate to join in such enjoyment? To enter into the spirit of the occasion?'

'Dunno. Depends, doesn't it?'

'On what, Mr Tring?'

'Well, I mean if he was with the gang an' that. The bike mob.'

'His friends, in short.'

'Well, I mean you go around, muck in, have a giggle, p'raps.'

'Exactly,' said Mr Plant-Huntleigh. He sounded pleased.

Delicately, the coroner intervened.

'Forgive me, but as the witness has no legal adviser with him here today, perhaps I might suggest he be asked forthwith if he was in the company of the deceased at the fair. He can scarcely be expected to help establish the circumstances if he was not.'

'I am obliged to you, sir,' said the barrister. 'My instructions, however, are that no witness of the accident has come forward and that the police have been unable to solicit assistance in the matter even from such companions of this unfortunate young man as are known to have been present in the fair at the time.'

Purbright half rose. 'That is so, sir.'

'In which case,' resumed Mr Plant-Huntleigh, 'I think I may fairly say, with respect, that a lack of direct evidence must enhance the value of what we may learn about the deceased, his personality and habits, from an informed, articulate and intelligent witness such as Mr Tring here.'

Sergeant Malley gave a silent whistle in admiration of the London lawyer's dazzling forensic mendacity. The witness, curling his lip, covertly sent a two-fingered signal to his friends and relations.

'Mr Tring,' said his champion, pleasantly, 'we have heard the nice things you said about Digger – his readiness to be a good mixer, his high spirits, his love of "having a giggle". Now, then, you must not be offended by this last question of mine. It has to be asked, you understand, and you should not regard it as an accusation. All I wish you to say is whether or not your brother was a drinking man.'

Mr Tring drew himself to full height and addressed the coroner, accompanied by a mutter of shocked rebuttal at the back of the court.

'Your Honour, as God's my judge, that boy never went inside a pub in all his life and I can fetch parsons who'll tell you that – parsons, not bloody policemen!'

'You sound, if I may say so, admirably confident in your brother's sobriety, Mr Tring,' observed Mr Plant-Huntleigh.

' 'Course I am.'

'So if, for the sake of argument, someone ever *did* persuade him to take alcohol . . .'

'What d'you mean, argument? Who's been arguing?'

The balm of Mr Plant-Huntleigh's smile flowed forth. His hand, like a guru's, enjoined peace. 'No, no, no, Mr Tring. I am putting to you an utterly imaginary situation. I am asking you – a sensitive and sensible person – what would be likely to happen if a teetotaller, a non-drinker, your late brother, for instance, were to be induced – against his will, perhaps – to imbibe alcoholic liquor.'

For a moment Tring pondered, frowning suspiciously. Then he shrugged.

'Well, he'd get pissed, wouldn't he?'

Mr Plant-Huntleigh, suddenly transformed back into a remote eminence, no longer the kindly confidant of bereaved storekeepers, made curt intimation to the coroner that he had no further questions, and moved his seat to confer with the whiskered man in green velveteen.

Dr Heineman was called.

The pathologist from Flaxborough General Hospital was a brisk enthusiast who gave his evidence in the manner of a lecturer. He was lithe and bony, with remarkably mobile eyebrows. In his gracefully gesticulating right hand was an invisible scalpel with which he seemed all the time to be parting and excising layers of tissue. It seemed a pity, Purbright reflected, that so professional a performance could, in the end, produce nothing better than a report of a common or garden busted skull.

'And that was the cause of death, was it, doctor?' asked the coroner, also sensible of anti-climax.

'Thet,' responded Dr Heineman, 'was the cows of dith. Igsectly.'

Mr Cannon looked inquiringly at Mr Plant-Huntleigh.

'If he would kindly reiterate one tiny point,' said the barrister, rising, 'I should be most obliged. Purely a matter of confirmation of my notes, doctor.'

Dr Heineman smiled an Old Vienna smile.

'Analysis of a sample of the blood of the deceased disclosed – am I correct? – an alcohol content equivalent to that which would be produced by consuming five ounces of spirits.'

'One handred end forty grems. Five wunces. Shoor.'

'A quarter of a bottle of whisky, doctor.'

'Yis. Thet you could say.'

'Thank you, doctor.'

It took some time for the import of this quiet, businesslike exchange to register upon the Tring family. When it did, they voiced indignation so forcefully that the coroner sent Malley to give them the choice between silence and eviction.

Mr Cannon then announced his intention of adjourning the inquest for two weeks.

'I think there would be no point in an adjournment *sine die*,' he said, looking directly at Mr Plant-Huntleigh as if seeking his permission to use such a very legal phrase. 'Police inquiries into the accident are proceeding, of course, but the view of the police is that if a witness does not come forward in the next week or so – while the fair is in the town, in fact – it must be considered unlikely that we shall ever know more than we do now about this unfortunate occurrence.'

'There is other testimony to be heard, though, is there not? Irrespective of what may or may not be offered by the hypothetical eye-witness.'

Mr Cannon hurriedly assured Counsel for the proprietor of Space Shot that there was indeed such testimony and that it would be put on record two weeks hence. Depositions had been taken from two fairground attendants and an engineer's report on the equipment from which the man had fallen would also be entered as evidence.

'I have a copy of that report,' said Mr Plant-Huntleigh. 'I think that in order to alleviate possible public anxiety I should be permitted to disclose that the ride known as Space Shot has been found to be absolutely safe.'

'Crafty sod,' murmured Malley to Purbright. 'I'll bet that's the swiftest two hundred quid he ever earned.'

The coroner said he considered Mr Plant-Huntleigh's application perfectly reasonable in the circumstances. Courteously, they bobbed at each other. Papers were gathered, chairs pushed back. Dr Heineman went bounding off towards his pickles and dissection slabs. Policemen loitered gravely, like museum attendants at closing time, until all the members of the public had departed; then they unbuttoned tunics and some lit cigarettes.

Chapter Three

IRREVERENCE WAS NOT A CHARGE THAT COULD FAIRLY be laid against Detective Sergeant Sidney Love. So when on one occasion he described life in the highly priced houses on Oakland as 'all single beds and dinner gongs', he was expressing genuine admiration.

Purbright found rather touching his sergeant's attitude to what he regarded as the symbols of social eminence. Love was quite without envy and it would never have occurred to him to concede, in the course of his job, any privilege to the wealthy. Rather was he, Purbright thought, a sort of amateur anthropologist, ready always to be happily surprised by discovery of such gewgaws of trivial chieftainship as a white telephone or a leopardskin lavatory seat cover.

'*Dinner* gongs?' the inspector had echoed, intrigued despite himself.

Love had flushed boyishly and added: 'Just little ones. On sideboards. I don't think they ring them any more.'

'Ah, vestigial gongs.'

David and Julia Harton, of Number Six Oakland, did not own a dinner gong, vestigial or otherwise, but they occupied single beds and had done for nearly two years.

It was the morning following the first stage of the inquest on Robert Digby Tring. Julia Harton had risen from her single bed and stood now, yawning, scratching her right knee, and looking out of the window, from which she had raised a flower-patterned yellow linen blind. David Harton lay in his single bed, with one arm behind his head. He regarded his wife's back with a lazy smile. By shifting his gaze very slightly, he was able to check on the smile in a mirror that covered half the wall opposite. The smile was his wry one. He nodded amiably to his reflection and looked again towards his wife.

Julia's head was bowed. She was frowning down at her hands. With one thumbnail she chiselled off little flakes of varnish from the nails of the other hand. The light from the window outlined the body within the thin nightdress, which was rumpled and caught up on one hip. It was a small body, sturdy at neck and wrist and ankle, but narrow chested and with fine arms and shoulders. The only evidence of fat was a puffiness at the very top of her thighs. Even her belly, distended by her attitude of sulky abstraction, had nothing pendulous about it.

'You're a pretty gross bitch,' David Harton remarked. 'Look, why don't you get a decent girdle or something?'

She glanced about her at the floor. It was littered with pieces of clothing: his, not hers. She reached forth one foot and hooked a pair of orange and green striped briefs on her toe. With a frown of distaste she tossed the briefs into a corner.

David followed the performance with his eyes, his smile unchanged.

Julia avoided looking at him directly, but she noticed that he had unbuttoned the jacket of his pyjamas. The froth of his chest hair was a dark blur in the outfield of her vision.

Without haste, she went about assembling her own outfit in readiness for dressing. She put everything neatly upon a white satin stool, then crossed to the chest of drawers where towels were kept. As usual, she would need a fresh one: David's final act at night invariably was to leave the bathroom and all its contents waterlogged.

She stooped to a drawer, easing it forth with alternating tugs and pushes. Its emergence was a reluctant waltz.

'Couldn't you even manage to fix a simple thing like this?' The question was quiet, weary, self-addressed. David pretended to consider it challenging. 'Christ, I told you, didn't I? Give Sandersons a ring. They'll see to it.'

'David, one does not call in a firm of building contractors to rub a bit of wax along a drawer runner.'

'Wax? Where does one get wax, for God's sake? What is the use of specialisation if fat-arsed women are too bloody stupid to make use of services that people have spent a lot of money and effort to provide?'

She took a towel from the drawer and put it on the floor beside her, then began unhurriedly to coax the drawer shut, using not her hands but her knees. The action imparted a sway to her body that would have seemed sexually provoking in other circumstances.

'Did you know,' David asked, sounding suddenly friendly and interested, 'that you can get a bra with a hole in each cup exactly seven-eighths of an inch in diameter and fringed with mongoose hair. It's supposed to be so stimulating that the nipples stand out permanently like nutmegs.'

Julia picked up the towel and straightened. She walked to the dressing table and gazed listlessly into its glass. In one corner of it she caught the reflection from the wall mirror of her husband. He had taken off his pyjamas and lay regarding his body with interest and approval.

She turned up her eyes in mock piety.

David spoke again. The tone continued to be light, conversational.

'They're starting these tactile expansion sessions at the Kissinger. Did you know?'

The Klub Kissinger, formerly the Floradora Club, on the outskirts of Flaxborough, offered health and psychiatric therapy service.

Julia said nothing.

'They might do you good. Why don't you go along?'

She paused, frowning. 'Tactile expansion?' Behind the scepticism and contempt was simple curiosity.

'You can be really dim, can't you?' He stroked one brown hairy thigh appreciatively. 'Expand – grow wider. Simple dictionary definition. Widen experience and knowledge. Tactile – by touch. Christ, didn't you go to school?'

On the dressing table was a jumble of jars, bottles and aerosol cans. Idly she picked out one of the cans. APPLE LOFT. Brings a Tang of the Country to the Man About Town.

'You mean it's a free-feel-for-all party?'

'You smug, middle-class cow.'

Julia smiled briefly at APPLE LOFT. 'You'll have to take your Bobby-May along, then, won't you?'

'It's you who need the therapy, love. It's your sex hang-up, not ours.'

At that 'ours' there was a slight stiffening of the woman's shoulders.

David noticed. He went on: 'You don't seem to realise how tiresome people find this small-town moral posturing of yours.'

'People? What people?' She had unscrewed a bottle of nail

lacquer and was ruminatively withdrawing the little brush attached to its stopper. Her back was still towards him.

'People who matter. Who happen to be important. You know perfectly bloody well.'

'Business mates.' She pronounced 'mates' with a kind of sardonic jauntiness.

Her husband raised himself suddenly on one elbow. 'Right,' he said emphatically. 'Business mates. Fine. And they make money, lots of money. Isn't that incredibly vulgar of them?'

Julia put a neat dab of nail lacquer on the nozzle of the APPLE LOFT can. Then she turned, collected her towel and clothing, and left without giving him another word or glance.

He remained still and listened to the slow, rustling drag of her slippers across the landing carpet. A door closed and was locked. The rest of the house was so silent that he could hear and identify the click of a dress button against wooden door panels, the brushing of chain across enamel, the creak of a tap.

David Harton's smile was no longer wry, as he could see in the mirror that he had had fitted in the days of higher nuptial expectation. It now bespoke pain, philosophically borne.

The distant gush of water ceased after four or five minutes. It was succeeded not by silence but by a faint, sustained vibrancy. Odd, how someone's presence in the bathroom always produced this subtle difference in the timbre of the house.

The woman was projected to him in a succession of tiny sounds. All had a muffled yet ringing quality, imparted by the tiled walls and the metallic drum belly of the bath. The echo of a discarded slipper striking the floor. A soft boom of weight travelling down through a naked heel. He heard the lick and swirl of water as she tested its warmth. The smile died quickly from his face.

Julia was bending low, half turned, and sweeping fanned fingers just below the surface. It was the same action as smoothing sand on a summer beach. The water lapped back into stillness. Fingers, glistening, converged upon the button at her throat, like wet bathers clustering at a tent. It was she now who smiled. Pensive, sensual amusement. She put first one hand, then the other into her nightdress's open front, wrists crossed, then slowly lifted her breasts up and apart within the hands' cupped caress. Her lower lip projected coquettishly. Slowly the hands turned, miming beneath the fabric the weight and fulness of their burden. Her body tensed and narrowed. The self-embracing arms tightened. The hands, suddenly stiff as surfboards, slid from breasts to shoulders and down, denuding them. She stepped into the bath as carefully as if before a critical audience, then gradually relaxed until she lay at full length, immersed just sufficiently for the tides born of her breathing to lap the white islands of her breasts and to suck her groin like currents in a seaweed grove.

There was a separate shower next to the bathroom. David used it energetically. The violent drubbing, arm-flailing and posturing beneath the needle-sharp onslaught of cold water he described as 'toning up'. Julia told her friends that he looked on these occasions like a discus thrower desperate for a pee.

David returned to the bedroom, leaving two pieces of soap, his pyjama trousers and two wet towels in the shower basin. Naked, he did eighteen press-ups on the floor in front of the mirror. Another towelling and a little muscular massage with finger tips. He examined his hands, turning fanned fingers this way and that. They were short and inclined to pudginess.

'Thornton! Thorney, darling!' Julia's voice from the landing. She had emerged from the bathroom to rouse their eight-year-old son, home on holiday from his boarding prep school.

The child, already up and dressed, answered from the kitchen where he was persuading Mrs Cutlock to feed him cake and cold tinned mushroom soup. Mrs Cutlock was the daily help. She had just arrived from her council house home in Simpson Road.

'Down soon, old chap!' cried Thornton's father, cheerily.

The whine of a vacuum cleaner signalled that Mrs Cutlock

was at large. David opened a couple of drawers and sorted their contents around until he found a pair of nylon briefs in silver and yellow checks, which he pulled on. Approvingly he adjusted the bulge produced by his genitals.

Julia entered, fully dressed. She glanced at the open drawers, the disturbed contents. Ignoring her husband completely, she sat for a moment before the dressing table and applied some makeup. She rose and walked towards the door.

'Julia . . .'

She stopped and waited, not looking at him.

'I'm seeing Weatherby today. I want to be able to tell him to go ahead with the divorce preparations.'

She said nothing.

'Did you hear what I said?'

Julia began to leave.

He grabbed her wrist and twisted it upward, into the small of her back. 'I said, did you hear? *Did you bloody hear?*'

On the staircase, the hoovering Mrs Cutlock had found an angle of observation through the banisters – a sort of leper's squint. She noted the raised voice and watched Mrs Harton suddenly double forward.

David was still smiling but there was a pale rigidity about his mouth. He pulled the woman close by holding her trapped wrist low, so that she had to crouch in an attitude of subservience.

'Now then, are you going to be reasonable?'

Mrs Cutlock saw Mrs Harton shake her head, then give a jerk. What, she asked the vacuum cleaner, could Mr and Mrs Harton be doing? Mrs Harton had jerked again. Surely Mr Harton wasn't kicking her? Oh, but yes, yes he was. With his bare foot. Short jabs with that big toenail of his. Poor Mrs Harton. Ooo – another one . . .

The involuntary grimaces of sympathy made by Mrs Cutlock were suddenly replaced by one of shocked wonderment as she saw Mr Harton reel backward, bent low and holding himself between his legs. The poor gentleman was white as a sheet, but she supposed it served him right. Who would have thought it of Mrs Harton, though? A headmaster's daughter. Grabbing her husband's balls. Quick as a terrier.

Julia crossed the landing and spent a couple of minutes more in the bathroom. When she emerged, she was singing.

Her voice was high and firm and possessed an almost professional accuracy of pitch. '*If you go down to the woods today* ...' The Teddy Bears' Picnic was Thornton's special favourite, or so it had been when he was four.

Mrs Cutlock stood aside on the stairs and grinned as Mrs Harton went by. Her employer did not interrupt her song, but in mid-note she made a bow of greeting, playfully arch, like a princess in musical comedy. Mrs Cutlock giggled and reflected that Mrs Harton was a cool one all right.

'*... for every bear that ever there was ...*'

David listened and scowled. He tossed a few things about until he found his watch. He strapped it on, taking care not to catch any of his profuse, black forearm hair in the gold linkage. The watch told him the date, temperature, air pressure, and could be used as a currency conversion calculator. Its mechanism was accurate to within two seconds in five years. David kept the watch quarter of an hour fast.

He picked up the APPLE LOFT deodorant, aimed at his left armpit and pressed the button. Nothing happened. He shook the can and tried again. He twisted the button and took different aim. The country-fresh tingle remained imprisoned within its man-size pack. David angrily wrenched the nozzle from side to side. Suddenly it came away. David's torso was hit by a stream of foaming APPLE LOFT like the contents of a fire extinguisher. It was searingly cold and of ghastly pungency.

His yell of shock and pain penetrated to the kitchen, where Julia was humming a reprise of The Teddy Bears' Picnic for Thornton's benefit while she broke eggs into a basin.

'Daddy's calling, darling,' she said. 'Go and see what he wants.'

Ten minutes later, David was dressed, composed, and seated with his son in the dining enclosure that was screened from cook top and sluice unit by rubber plants and shelves of spice jars.

'Mummy was in good voice this morning, wasn't she?'

Thornton, a frail boy with ash-blond hair, looked at his father, then at his mother. His eyes were wary.

Julia took off to the tap the saucepan in which she had scrambled eggs.

David began buttering a piece of toast. He cleared his throat. 'This singing business . . .' He waited for Julia to come back to the table and sit down. 'This singing – does it betoken bliss?' David glanced at the child, as though inviting him to learn something.

'A sort of resolute cheerfulness?' David persisted. He reached for marmalade, then, seeming to notice for the first time the egg on the plate before him, he pushed the jar aside. He loaded his fork with egg.

'We have to be resolute, don't we, darling?' Julia said to Thornton. The boy smiled at his plate.

'Humming I can understand,' David said. 'That's spontaneous. You hum sometimes, don't you, Thornton?'

'Sometimes.'

'There's a big difference, though, between humming and giving a recital at the top of one's voice. Do you remember the woman you heard at that concert we took you to?'

'Rather!' said Thornton. 'I saw all the way down into her mouth!' For a moment he grinned happily.

'Daddy was asleep most of the time,' Julia said. 'The lady must have seen all the way down into his mouth, too. I hope his tongue didn't have its whisky overcoat on, don't you?' She sounded fond and confidential.

Thornton glanced at his father and giggled uncertainly.

'Singing,' David told him, 'is a rather queer thing. You'll see what I mean if you keep your eyes open, old chap. Singers –

those who make a habit of it, I mean – are all ugly. All of them. The throat muscles become unnaturally developed, you see. Their necks get to look like – oh, I don't know – like . . . like athletes' thighs!'

Julia, composedly pouring herself a cup of coffee, caught Thornton stealing a guilty look at her throat and smiled at him.

'Your daddy,' she said, 'is very fastidious about keeping thighs in their right place.'

'I rather suspect, you know,' said David to the forkful of scrambled egg that he was assembling, 'that your mother has musical ambitions. I've never heard quite so much night starvation sublimated into the Teddy Bears' Picnic before.'

Thornton decided he had been given a cue to be funny. 'Were you really starving all night, Mummy?'

Julia smiled at him. 'He *is* a funny old daddy, isn't he? Actually, *he's* the one who gets peckish in bed, but even daddies have to learn that there's a time and place for everything.'

David ate his meal hastily, but with close attention to the texture of the scrambled egg, most of which seemed to fail whatever test he was applying because he shunted it into separate piles around the rim of his plate and left it. He took bites from three slices of toast but finished none.

Thornton watched, making no start on his own food. When his father rose and went noisily through the hallway to the lobby, the child slipped down from the table and opened the back door.

David reappeared wearing a short suede car coat and a flat peaked cap in pink plastic.

'Oh, Christ!' murmured Julia. 'We're off to Disneyland.'

He strode through, ignoring her.

Thornton was latching back the long wrought-iron gate at the end of the drive. He already had opened the garage doors.

His father climbed into the big green Hastings-Pumari, grinned at the boy and made a gallant aviator sort of sign with one thumb. 'Okay, old chap – chocks away!' He transferred the thumb to the starter button. The car gave a forward lurch, as if in pained alarm.

David scowled, wrenched it out of gear, and again pushed the starter button. He held it in for nearly half a minute. The engine failed to fire. The pulsating, grinding laughter of the starter motor brought Julia to the kitchen window. She smirked blandly.

The boy came running to the car. David tried to ask him who the hell had been playing with the thing but Thornton did not listen. 'Choke!' he was shouting. 'Have you got the choke out?'

David glared at the dashboard. Choke. That one. No, he hadn't. Confused, he switched off the ignition. The boy looked over his shoulder.

'You've not switched on!' It was a cry of surprise, of delight, of triumph.

'If ever I catch you touching this bloody car again . . .'

Open-mouthed, winded by injustice, Thornton stepped back and pressed himself against the garage wall. The big car drew out and sped erratically towards the gateway.

Ten minutes later, the postman had brought the morning mail and Thornton was soothing his wounded pride with sachets of the Instant Old English Ginger Beer for which he had persuad d his mother to rush a coupon seven weeks previously.

For Julia there came in the same little pile of packets and envelopes an offer of comfort of a very different kind.

She read the letter through once, twice, three times. She examined it carefully. Then she read it again.

Finally, after making sure that Thornton was happily pre-occupied and that Mrs Cutlock had descended into the area of table clearing and washing up, Julia went to her bedroom. She locked the door and sat down by the extension telephone. After long deliberation she picked up the receiver and dialled a Flaxborough number.

Response was almost immediate.

'My name,' she said, 'is Mrs Harton. Mrs Julia Harton, of Oakland.'

'Ah, yes. Mrs Harton. Splendid.' The voice was cultured, friendly – avuncular, almost.

'You wrote to me.'

'I did, indeed. And you have responded. I do hope you are free for lunch.'

'Who are you?' She tried to sound cold and incurious.

'I did sign the letter, Mrs Harton. Don't tell me that the old professional affectation hasn't been quite subdued yet. A sign of immaturity, alas.'

'Affectation?'

'Illegibility. Prescriptions no one can read. You know?'

Prescriptions. Was he a doctor then? She didn't ask, for fear of sounding naive.

'I take it,' she said instead, 'that this letter of yours is supposed to be some kind of a joke.'

He chuckled softly, and with no hint of resentment. 'Why should you think that?'

'Oh, come now, Mr . . .'

'Rothermere. Mortimer Rothermere.'

'. . . Mr Rothermere. It is your letter-heading which I assumed was meant to be funny. What are you – a pop group or something?'

Again the unoffended chuckle. 'Nothing so bizarre, I assure you. Unfortunately, honest trade descriptions are sufficiently rare nowadays as to sound melodramatic.'

Julia was beginning to find the urbanity of Mr Rothermere challenging. Very seldom among her husband's friends and visitors was she able to converse in a way that she considered did justice to her own education and natural intelligence. David associated almost exclusively with people from outside Flaxborough – bankers, property men and some rather odd characters he called efficiency consultants: all conversational cripples unless money or golf were the topic.

'Yes, but really! The name of this set-up of yours – I ask you!' And she gave the sort of creamy laugh that she remembered as characteristic of a Girton tutor who had made her feel much ashamed of an essay of hers on Dickens the Great Reformer. 'What's the "Inc." for, anyway? I know Americans stick it after everything but I've no idea what it stands for.'

A little purr of good humour, then: 'Strictly speaking, Incorporated. But we rather like to think' – another purr – 'Incarnate.'

After a pause, Julia asked: 'How did you come to know those things about us – about me and my husband?'

'Lunch, Mrs Harton . . . it will be so much more satisfactory. Have you any preferences?'

She pouted thoughtfully, then turned to look at the little china clock on the table beside her bed. When she spoke again, her 'Very well, Mr Rothermere,' was terse and cool. She asked: 'Do you know a restaurant in Spoongate called Fold's?'

'I do, indeed.'

'Oh, please don't sound enthusiastic on my account. The food is mediocre and the prices preposterous. My husband happens to have an account there, that's all.'

'I must say I rather like your sense of fitness, Mrs Harton. Of occasion. We shall get along famously, never fear.'

'Twelve forty-five,' she said. 'The head waiter will be able to point me out. Unless, of course, I don't bother to pursue this nonsense any further.'

And she rang off.

Chapter Four

FIRST FRUIT OF THE PUBLICITY ACCORDED THE TRING inquest by the East Midlands *Evening Gazette* fell into Inspector Purbright's office in the shape of Miss Patricia Booker.

'I thought you ought to hear what she has to say,' said Sergeant Malley, to whom, as Coroner's Officer, the girl had been referred from the inquiries counter downstairs.

In the fatherly shade of Bill Malley, Purbright saw a plump-faced girl of about sixteen, who nodded to him familiarly and then made a quick and manifestly unimpressed survey of the room. She sat in the chair brought forward for her by Malley.

'This accident at the fair,' she said, then was silent.

Purbright waited. Just as it began to seem that Patricia intended the verbless fragment to stand as a complete exposition, she added:

'Me and a friend was in Venus.'

'One of the cars,' Malley explained to the inspector. 'On that roundabout thing. They're all named after stars or planets or something.'

Patricia's large, healthy eyes shone. 'Twenty-eight times me and my friend's been up. Fabulous. Venus is best. You know. Clean.'

'Clean?'

'Yeah, well, I mean some of them's been thrown up in. You know.'

The inspector intimated that he did know, yessir.

Suddenly the girl was solemn.

'This fellow. The dead one. We saw him fall out.' She stared up over her shoulder at Malley, then at Purbright.

'Hurms is just in front of Venus,' she said. Purbright hoped the sergeant would not fuss over the mispronunciation, but all Malley said to him was: 'That's the one Tring was in. Hurms.'

'They'd been larking about,' said Patricia. 'Inside the module. I mean you're supposed to be strapped in, aren't you? And it turns over, doesn't it?' She fanned all ten fingers over her stomach, looked up at the ceiling and gasped dramatically.

'Tell the inspector what you mean by larking about.'

'Well, showing off, actually. You know. I think they must have spotted me and my friend.'

'There were two men in the car, were there?' Purbright felt it was time to get the narrative into some sort of shape.

'Yeah. Like I said.'

'Ah, yes.'

'One of them kept leaning right over like he was on a horse or something. Or his bike. Could have been. I mean they was in leathers. And he was drinking out of a bottle, wasn't he? They both was taking drinks out of it but him specially. The other fellow never leaned about or nothing. He didn't really let go of his seat, did he? Not that I could see, he didn't. He wasn't such a show-off as the first fellow, the one that fell out.'

There was a long pause. Malley prompted. 'The door, Patricia. What was it you told me about the door?'

'Oh, yeah; the door. Well, that was funny. Just before all the modules started turning over and over, it came open. I could see it sort of flapping, couldn't I? And I said to Di, hey Di, those blokes have got their door open. But she wouldn't look because I think she was scared. And straight after that we started to turn over and I shut my eyes.'

'Were *you* scared, then?' Purbright asked.

'Me? No, shutting your eyes helps to make everything go dur-reamy,' and Patricia illustrated the condition there and then. She looked, the inspector thought, passably ecstatic.

'You didn't see how – in what manner – the door of the module in front came to be open?'

'No. It just was. And then it wasn't any more. I mean, that's what was funny about it really.'

Malley saw Purbright's understandable confusion. 'What you're telling us, Patricia, is that when you looked again, when you'd stopped turning over, the door of the car in front was fastened properly, like all the others. Is that right?'

She nodded. 'Yeah, and there was just this one bloke sitting inside. Straight up, like nothing had happened.'

'Wait a minute, Patricia.' Purbright was frowning. 'You

said earlier that you saw Mr Tring – one of the two men in front of you – fall out.'

'Well, he must have, mustn't he? I mean, there was two, then there was just one. He must have.'

'But you didn't actually see it happen?'

A momentary sulkiness clouded her face. 'I had my eyes shut, didn't I?'

'Ah, yes, of course. I'd forgotten.'

Miss Booker understood and forgave. After all, the tall and easy-going and nicely mannered policeman was quite good looking for his age – almost dishy in a sort of way. She would be able to tell Di and Linda and Trish that she was glad to have accepted their dare because now she was an important witness and would get her name in the *Flaxborough Citizen* and perhaps even the *Gazette*. And that would be dur-reamy.

The inspector put a few more questions in a style more conversational than investigatory. Then Malley shepherded the girl away to the tiny office in the basement where, with frowns and wheezes and slow, one-fingered diligence, he would translate her story into a typed deposition.

Purbright and Malley met later. With the inspector was Detective Sergeant Love. Purbright indicated him and said to Malley: 'Sid here has been much abused by Grandma Tring.'

'Who hasn't.'

'Quite. But in this case her complaint is specific and a bit odd.'

Love spoke. 'She says that somebody's pinched a photograph of Digger.'

Malley looked up from the short, black pipe he had been probing with a piece of wire. 'I'd have thought the only photograph of anybody in that family had been taken by us. Profile and full face.'

'I don't think she was telling the tale,' Love said. 'She said a reporter had called a couple of days ago – at least, he said he was a reporter – and she answered a lot of questions about her grandson. Then he asked for a picture of him so that the picture could be printed with the story. She gave him a framed photograph of Digger with his bike.'

'So?' Malley was busy again with his pipe.

'It's the frame the old lady's bothered about,' said Love. 'She says it's silver.'

Malley smiled knowingly, but said nothing.

Love looked at Purbright, as if for support against the unconscionable scepticism of the Coroner's Officer.

'The point is,' said the inspector, 'that nobody from the *Citizen* office has been anywhere near the Tring household. When the old woman called and demanded to have her photo back, they didn't know what she was talking about and pushed her on to us.'

'Me, actually,' complained Love.

'What's the crime – larceny of a picture frame?'

Malley blew down the newly excavated pipe stem. There was a noise like a death rattle and a sudden, overpowering reek of tar.

Purbright looked thoughtfully at Patricia Booker's deposition. The signature, in painstaking back-sloped script, had a childish flourish at the end.

'Tring's companion on that ride seems to have been a remarkably self-possessed character,' said the inspector. 'I like the way this kid remembers seeing him after the roll – "sitting straight up like nothing had happened".'

Malley snorted amiably. 'Aye, well, they're all pretty hard buggers, that lot.'

'Even so, when your mate's just gone out into a fifty-foot dive on to concrete, I should scarcely suppose your first instinct would be to shut the door after him and sit tight.'

'They aren't very easy to close, those doors,' Love informed them. 'I tried all of them. The latches are very strong.'

'You've seen the engineer's report, have you?' Purbright asked.

33

Love and Malley said they had. It was mainly a lot of technical bumf but there was no doubt the equipment was in good order. 'Better than some public transport,' averred Love, in daring disregard of The Establishment, as represented by the Flaxborough and District Passenger Committee and its eight buses.

'So you'd rule out the possibility of that particular door coming open on its own – or rather being swung open by the motion of the car.'

Love confirmed that he would. He showed in mime the way the latch was secured, then freed.

Having watched, the inspector said: 'I'm afraid I had assumed up to now that the door could have been opened quite easily by accident – by a drunk knocking against it, for instance.'

'Oh, no; he'd have to get hold of the latch handle properly and give it those three separate pulls and pushes.' Again Love demonstrated in mid-air.

Malley said: 'It doesn't follow that just because Tring had had a few drinks he couldn't get a door open.'

'Deliberately, yes,' said Purbright, 'but I was talking about his doing it by accident.'

'All those Trings are mad sods,' observed Malley. 'Them and the Cutlocks and the O'Shaunessys. Why shouldn't he have opened it deliberately?'

'Bravado?'

'Showing off. Certainly, why not? There were a couple of totties just behind.'

Purbright glanced quickly down the girl's deposition in search of a remembered phrase, found it, frowned.

'She says she recognised Digger Tring but not the other one because "he kept his lid shut".' He looked up. 'His motor cycling helmet, I presume?'

'That's right.'

' "Shut" though – what does that mean?'

Love explained. 'She's talking about the visor. It's a shield of dark coloured plastic that comes right down over the face.'

'Hinged,' added Malley. 'Digger would have to push his up out of the way because he was drinking, remember.'

'Ah, yes. Neat whisky. And a rather superior brand.'

Across Malley's big moon face flitted good-natured suspicion. He raised his eyebrows.

'It's all right, Bill; there's probably no connection. But the conscientious Johnson did find a smashed bottle near the West Row corner when they were collecting Tring. A Glenmurren straight malt, no less.'

'Digger,' said Love, 'couldn't have told the difference between whisky and fly spray.'

The inspector acknowledged his own impression that the Tring family appetites were not noticeably selective.

'He could always have pinched it, of course,' conceded Malley, and with this reasonable hypothesis the matter of the whisky was abandoned.

Which is not to say that Inspector Purbright had gained from his exchange with Malley and Love any substantial degree of assurance that he would be able to conceal, during an impending and unavoidable interview with the Chief Constable, that instinctive unease which Mr Chubb found so irksome a quality in his detective inspector.

Chapter Five

MORTIMER ROTHERMERE BACKED THE BIG LEMON coloured Fiat into a space in the centre of a line of cars in a private yard behind the Education Committee offices. He parked it with a single confident sweep, looking back and giving the wheel the precise final three-quarters turn that would just leave him room to open the door without risk to the adjacent Daimler.

A porter limped from a doorway. He leaned a little to one side so that the sleeve of his uniform hung low, concealing his hand. From the end of the sleeve a blue thread of smoke escaped.

Rothermere fished a brief case, a furled umbrella and *The Times* from the back of the car and swung the door shut. He patted his curly-brimmed, silver-grey homburg and prepared to cross the yard.

'Can't park there, sir,' announced the porter. 'That's the Director's place.'

'My good man, you don't have to tell *me*. I *am* the Director.'

The porter faltered. He had put one hand behind his back. 'Yes, but Mr Parry . . .'

'Dismissed.' Rothermere, though brusque, sounded regretful. 'They should have told you.'

He strode past the porter, entered the door, turned right along a corridor, crossed the hall into which it led, and left the building by its main entrance in Southgate. On his way to Fold's, some twenty yards distant, Rothermere noted with approval that street parking was prohibited throughout the area.

Julia Harton had arrived early at the restaurant in order to study, away from Mrs Cutlock's heavily suggestive solicitude and the demands of a Thornton already bored with holidays and impatient to return to school on the morrow, the curious communication from Happy Endings Inc.

She sniffed musingly the medicinal tingle of the bubbles bursting from her double Campari and soda, and read:

You have been selected, on the recommendation of persons of financial probity and social eminence, who work as a voluntary body to advise this organisation, as a suitable candidate for assistance and support by Happy Endings Inc.

Our Confidential Research Division experts have already examined data relevant to your case, and I am delighted to be able to tell you they have decided that your high Community Rating merits the offer of a very special service – that of our Cliveden Bureau.

The Cliveden Bureau operates as a general rule for the exclusive benefit of titled selectees. Some of the country's oldest families have been enabled by the Bureau to make matrimonial readjustments without fuss or scandal, and it has long enjoyed their confidence and gratitude. Now you, Mrs Harton, because of the delicacy of your social connections, and the necessity of avoiding scandal that might weaken your husband's commercial standing (and hence his capacity to compensate you adequately for the dissolution of your marriage), may share with the greatest in the land the privilege of Benefit without Bother.

Terms, of course, are an immaterial consideration in the context of the work of Happy Endings Inc., but we would assure you at the outset that a minimal percentage – a mere out-of-pocket reimbursement – is the total of our expectation.

All you need do in order to take advantage of this offer is to telephone the undersigned at Flaxborough 2229. He has the pleasure of being the representative appointed to be especially responsible for your interests.

For the next quarter of an hour, Julia sipped her drink and idly amused herself by comparing each new arrival with her mental picture of Mortimer Rothermere. Most of the diners could be disqualified at once; they were local business or professional men known to her, at least by sight. As Julia had expected, none was accompanied by a wife at this time of day. Her assignation might be noticed, but it would not be diligently monitored.

At last the door was pushed open in the confident, but not quite brash, manner exactly suitable to the entry of a man with broad shoulders, a greying but impeccably trimmed beard that emphasised his rosiness of cheek, an eye bright and watchful yet calm, and a big expanse of brow beneath the sort of hat that kings used to wear to race meetings.

He had an air, Julia decided. He had tone. Moreover, even if there was a hint of corsetry about him, he was not at all bad looking. She hoped very much that he was Mr Rothermere.

And so he was. But for some moments he remained where he stood, just inside the restaurant's entrance, peering vaguely into the pink dusk of the long, narrow room.

Five years before, Fold's had been a homely, slightly shabby eating house; its glass-topped tables a-clatter with cruets and thick tumblers and much worn cutlery with ornate, cast metal handles, each with a tiny drainage hole out of which vestiges of washing-up water would trickle upon the wrists of the unwary. In those days ('I think I'll have the beef, Miss, and the apple crumble to follow . . .') the ordinariness of the food had been honestly proclaimed in the light from high, naked windows. Now, though, the windows were darkened; some were masked in heavy velvet, others turned into alcoves, shallowly shelved to display culinary whimsicalities – a pepper mill, an old enamelled herb jar, a copper ladle. What light there was came from thickly shaded sconces. It was just enough to convey the prices on the menu as impressions rather than statements. It was a blush of well-being; a subtle reminder to the beneficiaries of Cultox Nutritionals (Catering Division) that spending money, unlike making it, carried the obligation of grace.

A shadow became flesh.

'Sah . . .' suspired the head waiter. He stood at Mr Rothermere's side, looking prepared not so much to serve him as to truss him up.

Mr Rothermere continued to stare down the room. One did not look at head waiters: direct regard would be abdication.

'Sah?' The man's face jerked upward; taut, helpful, insolent. 'Mrs Harton, I believe, is lunching here.' Mr Rothermere took a gold watch from his waistcoat and frowned at it, as if to invite the commemoration of this particular minute snatched from an unimaginably busy day.

The head waiter reached into the air and snapped a little of it between finger and thumb.

One of the floor waiters materialised from the gloom.

'Table six,' said the head waiter. He glanced distastefully at Mr Rothermere's brief case and umbrella. The subordinate put out his hand. 'Might I, sir?'

Ignoring him, Mr Rothermere turned and began walking past tables. The waiter had almost to run to overtake him and to become, with bobs and napkin flutterings, the dancing partner of the pulled-out chair.

Mrs Harton watched over the top of her glass. She inclined her head very slightly. Mr Rothermere gave her a full bow before taking his seat. Then, for four or five seconds, he gazed upon her with every appearance of fond approval.

'You look,' said Mrs Harton, 'just like Edward the Seventh.'

Mr Rothermere chuckled delightedly. With plump, white fingertips he patted and caressed his moustache. Julia noticed how small and pink was the mouth framed by all the carefully groomed whisker-work.

The mutual examination was interrupted by the descent before each of a menu the size of a card table.

Julia returned hers at once without looking at it. She ordered a cheese omelette, a little salad and French bread. From behind the other menu came cautiously the voice of Mr Rothermere. He asked for translations of some of the more ecstatic prose passages. The waiter – also, it seemed, a stranger to menu language – met each inquiry with the earnest assurance that the comestible indicated was 'very nice, sir.'

Resignedly, Mr Rothermere gave the signal for the menu to be hauled up. 'It had better be the sweetbreads.' He held up a hand in a delicate measuring gesture. 'Very few mushrooms. And no potatoes.'

Julia now saw that her companion had assumed a pair of gold-rimmed half spectacles. They gave him an even more benign appearance. 'Whenever I see a bill of fare like that,' he said to her, 'I can hear the dull thud of the freezer lid and the whine of the infra-red resuscitator. We live in wicked times, Mrs Harton.'

Julia regarded him for a moment. 'You sound like a moralist, Mr Rothermere.'

Quickly he shook his head. 'Moralising is like refrigeration. It doesn't make life any better; just destroys the flavour.'

'My husband,' she said, 'might almost be said to be an *im*moralist. He is for ever talking like a rake, but the only real talent he has is one for making money.'

'You resent that?'

'His talk or his talent?'

'His money-making.'

'Not in the least. One must love somebody to resent his preoccupations. The talk, though, I do find a bore. It's meant to be provocative, of course.'

The wine list had arrived. While looking through it rapidly for what he wanted, Mr Rothermere held his free hand in a gesture of postponement of all other matters. The hand, Julia noticed, was white and very clean. The fingers were short and thick. On the backs of the fingers grew symmetrical patches of ginger hair. He wore three rings, one jewelled.

'The fifty-nine Macon.' He handed back the list. To Julia he said: 'He probably is fearful of impotence. That troubles rich men quite a lot, actually.'

'All David fears is that I'll . . .'

She stopped, looking suddenly surprised, as if the absurdity of the situation had only just occurred to her. From her handbag she drew the letter she had received.

'Look here, just what *is* all this about?' She smoothed out the sheet of paper and peered first at it, then at him, shaking her head. 'I must be out of my bloody mind.'

Mr Rothermere mournfully chewed a fragment of roll while he watched delivery of steaks and fried potatoes to three silent, wary men at a nearby table. They eyed the meat on their plates like secret policemen counting in a new batch of suspects.

'Nonsense, my dear,' Mr Rothermere assured her in an abstracted manner. 'You are here because you think I can help you . . . God, just look at all that cholesterol . . . which of course I can.' He wrenched his regard away from the steaks and smiled at her with fully restored attention.

'Now then, tell me if I am wrong. You are married to a man of substance but no sensibility. He is boring, offensive and – worst of all – mean. You would be glad to let him have the divorce he so ardently desires for certain squalid purposes of his own. However, you would require adequate compensation for the loss of material comfort and social status which the marriage confers – or ought to confer. And you fear that your husband's meanness, in alliance with his own financial cunning and the expertise of his advisers, might result in your being cheated once you agree to start divorce proceedings. Am I correct?'

'Absolutely.' Julia's eyes had widened a fraction. 'You actually sound like a lawyer.'

Mr Rothermere's little pink lips pouted with pleasure. A ringed finger passed in and about his beard. 'I hate to think,' he said, 'that so expensively acquired a qualification should be obtrusive enough to be instantly detected.' He shrugged self-deprecatingly.

Food arrived.

Julia viewed her salad. Not a doctor, then. A lawyer. Not that he'd actually *said* . . .

'You could have him done away with,' remarked Mr Rothermere, in a matter-of-fact tone. 'He sounds as though he deserves it.' He speared a morsel of food on his fork. Julia was finding his beard not the least intriguing of the day's novelties;

she watched the piece of sweetbread conveyed through the hirsute hazard with quite remarkable deftness.

Airily, Mr Rothermere waved his fork. 'I was joking, of course.'

'Naturally.'

They tried some of the wine. Julia liked it very much, and said so. He topped up her glass immediately.

They ate. After a while Julia asked: 'This set-up of yours – is it something to do with *Reader's Digest*?'

'Good heavens, whatever makes you ask that?' His surprise was so complete that several seconds went by before he saw, and acknowledged with a grin, that the question had been sardonic.

'American Express?' she persisted. '*Encyclopedia Britannica*?' She tapped the letter with her knife. 'It's this privilege lark – the old you-have-been-selected approach. Oh dear.'

'You think it is fraudulent?' He broke off a piece of roll and began to butter it. 'I'm very glad you do. A client of intelligence is always much easier to work with.' He raised his eyes. 'Intelligence, and a modicum of ruthlessness.'

'Oh, I can be ruthless, all right.'

'Good. Now I shall tell you something surprising. The claims you so rightly view with scepticism happen to be true. You *have* been recommended – *and* selected. No come-on, Mrs Harton. It is all, as I believe the expression runs nowadays, happening for you.'

Julia watched the rosy cheeks broaden, the eyes crease into shining slits and the mouth tighten and tremble with amusement as Mr Rothermere suddenly gave himself up to a transport of good humour: a condition which he emphasised by seizing the bottle and filling their glasses with a flourish that even Dr Heineman could scarce have improved upon.

'I still don't understand,' she said. 'Why me? And who has been doing the recommending?'

A sudden cloud of regret dimmed his smile. 'My dear Mrs Harton, confidentiality is the essence of our organisation. You must see that.'

'It wasn't Daddy, was it?' she persisted. 'He's a Mason.'

'I'm sorry.'

'What, that he's a Mason?'

'That I cannot satisfy your perfectly natural curiosity.'

'It must be Daddy. He gets fits of indulgence. And he's always looked on David as a sort of Steerforth who ought to be expelled.' She giggled. 'By Christ, he's right, too.'

The waiter closed in. He partitioned them with menus. Julia said she wanted only black coffee. Mr Rothermere did some reading.

'Kindly tell me,' he said at last, 'what is meant by "couched in double Devon farmhouse cream, with mist of Kümmel and Toasted Kent hazels, dredged with rough-crushed Barbados crystals." '

'Sir?' The waiter leaned and peered at the description indicated by Mr Rothermere's finger. 'Oh, the strawberries, sir. Yes, they're very nice.'

Mr Rothermere said that coffee would suffice. Oh, and perhaps another bottle of wine.

'And now we shall never know,' he said to Julia. For the first time since their meeting, she gave him a full and friendly smile.

'No,' she said. 'So let us talk instead of my loathsome husband and how to make his life a misery. Not that we shall be able to. He is one of those asbestos bastards who are so convinced of their own marvellousness that you can be gouging their eyes out and they'll think it's because you want to go to bed with them.'

Mr Rothermere raised one finger. 'But money. That is different. That is their zone of sensitivity.'

'David's?'

'Oh, I think so.'

She shrugged. 'Maybe. I've never had a chance to kick him really hard in that area.'

Mr Rothermere regarded her narrowly. 'Twenty thousand pounds . . . do you suppose he would feel that?'

'God almighty!' Her sudden harsh laughter brought glances from the stolid steak-eaters. She paid no attention to them.

'Our inquiries indicate that twenty thousand would be just about the maximum he'd pay.'

'For a divorce?'

'He wishes to marry – or so I understand – a young woman called Lintz . . .'

Julia's amusement again got out of hand. 'Bobby-May!' she managed to gasp.

'That name I was told but did not believe. Now I suppose I shall have to.'

'Perfectly true, it really is. The whole family has a sort of tennis fixation. It comes out in the queerest ways.'

'Your husband,' he reminded her. 'There will have to be pressure, of course.'

'If you're serious about that twenty thousand, you're going to need boiling oil, never mind pressure.'

Mr Rothermere smiled blandly. 'Oh, I don't think so, Mrs Harton. Conventional, non-violent pressure will suffice, if there is enough of it.'

'Blackmail, do you mean?'

'I most certainly do not. Blackmail might be defined as seeking profit from a threat to disclose. The plan the Bureau has in mind in Mr Harton's case will operate on the opposite principle.'

Julia peered uncertainly into her glass. 'That sounds terribly complicated. You must' – with one finger she made little circles in the air – 'unravel it for me.'

'But of course. What we intend is simply to qualify for your husband's gratitude by rescuing him from an extremely unpleasant situation.'

'Rescuing him?'

'Yes. If he wishes us to. And guarantees that little settlement of twenty thousand pounds on the dissolution of your marriage.'

'And the situation you have in mind?' The finger now was picking out notes upon an imaginary keyboard. 'How unpleasant?'

'One of considerable pressure. But not exerted by us, so you need have no qualms, Mrs Harton.'

'By whom, then?'

'By experts, naturally. By the police.'

Julia looked blank. For a few moments, Mr Rothermere regarded her with a kind of twinkling speculation. Then suddenly he beamed and leaned forward.

'On which night this week would it be convenient for you to disappear, Mrs Harton?'

Julia's face remained impassive. She reached out her glass and held it while Mr Rothermere poured into it more wine. She sipped very slowly, waiting for him to expand the joke, but he said nothing. He was looking now at her shoulders and the rise of her breasts.

The silence, not the scrutiny, irritated her. She lowered her hand. 'Go on, then; let's hear the big strategy.'

For a few seconds more, his gaze was fixed upon the opening of Julia's dress with a steadiness that somehow turned the examination into a compliment. Then he sighed, leaned back in his chair and signalled the waiter. He ordered Benedictine.

'With such a throat,' he said to Julia, 'you deserve jewels. What does your husband spend his money on? Golf clubs, I suppose.'

She smiled, pleased. 'I think it's time you came to the point, Mr Rothermere.'

'Enough formality. Mortimer is my name.'

Julia made a little bow. 'Go on, then, Mortimer.'

'The plan?'

'But of course. The plan. The grand strategy.'

'Not here, I think. Perhaps my chambers. Would you be agreeable?'

Her laughter spilled tipsily. 'Chambers! Marvellous! And I'll bet you have etchings.'

'Alas, no longer. My second wife purloined the collection while I was in Helsinki.'

'I suppose you want me to ask what you were doing in Helsinki?'

He shrugged lightly. 'Embassy. One cannot take everything.'

'How true.'

'Curiously enough . . .' The liqueurs had just been placed on the table, and Mr Rothermere was regarding their golden gleam dreamily. 'Curiously enough, it was Helga – my third wife – who tried to make me a Benedictine addict. She regarded it as a sort of private love potion and made me drink a glass every night after dinner. "For your rheumatism, darling." Sweet. I mean, when have I ever had rheumatism? She was a Finn, of course. They think everyone else in the world is impotent. It was terribly funny one night – well, morning, actually – I remember it was light enough to see her hand when she raised it, with her fingers spread out – like that. "Oh, darling," she said, "I've been counting, and that was five times! You must never, never let yourself catch rheumatism!" So sweet . . . I always pretended it was the Benedictine; you know – just to please her.'

'Mortimer, you are a very gallant fellow.'

Mr Rothermere wrinkled his nose and screwed up his eyes in a fat-cat smile of satisfaction.

'I am, dear Julia, nothing of the kind. I am what your intelligence has divined already – an unprincipled scoundrel much given to venery and the taking of purses. You will see me yet in the Honours List. But' – he raised and wagged a plump finger – 'this I tell you quite seriously: if you really want this precious husband of yours beaten to his knees, you are going to have to match his unscrupulousness with some-thing like mine.'

'You are not really so wicked as you pretend.'

'Ah, you are preparing yourself for disappointment. There is no need.'

'It is you who may be disappointed.'

He made a small gesture of deprecation; gold and a jewel glinted in the flurry of white fingers.

'In my chambers,' he said, impishly confiding, 'I believe there remains a nearly full bottle of Madeira wine. Let us go and lay our scheme.'

Sleepily and happily acquiescent, she shrugged and looked about her for the handbag she supposed she had brought with her some – how many? – hours before. Was it only that morn-ing the ridiculous letter had arrived? From Mortimer. Dapper Mortimer with the curly brimmed hat and the boulevardier's air. Happy Endings, for god's sake. Ah, well, she'd had a bath – that was for sure – and changed into fresh pants. Roll on ye spheres of destiny ...

She jerked herself properly awake. The waiter was by her side, offering her a scrap of paper on a tray. He kept his distance, as if the paper was infectious. It was only the bill. Without examining it, she scribbled her signature on one corner. The waiter withdrew.

'David's bunch own this place,' she said. 'Wouldn't you just know it?'

'There is, I agree, a sort of logic in the connection between a restaurant and a dog food factory. One cannot help being put in mind of Sweeney Todd and the pie shop.'

Julia laughed but shook her head. 'Pure coincidence, I'm afraid. Cultox have got their greedy hands on so many things that nobody knows who's running what or where.' She waved a hand. 'All this ... I mean, what genius of an accountant thought that hard-headed, civilised country people who love their bellies would fall for this sort of rubbish?'

Mr Rothermere made no reply. He sat on, looking patiently benevolent and flicking the occasional crumb from his own, presumably well loved, belly.

Julia, too, lapsed into silence. She bowed her head. Mr Rothermere watched her fingering absently a button on the front of her dress. When she spoke at last, it was quietly and with only a hint of difficulty that the last glass or two of wine had induced.

'David is a real twenty-four carat Cultox-brand pig. All I want is to hear him squeal while he has his bank account cut. I'd say throat, but he's got no nerves in that.'

Mr Rothermere nodded. He rose from the table and stepped to the back of Julia's chair, ready to draw it out for her.

'We shall have to see,' he said, 'just what we can devise along those lines.' He patted, then squeezed, her shoulder. 'I have high hopes, I really have.'

Chapter Six

MR ROTHERMERE'S 'CHAMBERS' PROVED TO BE A CHALET in the Oxby Moor Motel, a mile west of Flaxborough. It held a large double divan, a combined chest of drawers and bureau, and a table with a telephone. Closet doors of simulated mahogany were set in one pale blue wall. On the wall facing the divan was a television set; it looked an integral part of the permanent structure. Through an open door Julia glimpsed lemon tiling, the edge of a wash basin, and some chromium plating.

She sat on the divan, leaning back on one elbow, and watched Rothermere fussily make disposition of hat, umbrella and briefcase. *The Times* he seemed to have left behind in the car. He closed the bathroom door after bringing out a basketwork chair. This he carried to the bureau and sat down.

From one of the drawers he took a notebook, a newspaper cutting and a camera. Julia wondered about Madeira, but it seemed that more urgent matters were to be disposed of first.

Mr Rothermere ran a thumb along his moustache, stroked his cheeks twice, made a sort of will-reading rumble in his throat, and began:

'We were never in doubt that we should use the classic ploy of the vanished wife in this case. Circumstances are unusually favourable. Your husband's factory has precisely the sort of machinery and disposal plant that would make your disappearance convincing. Add to the annoyance of being placed in peril of a murder charge the catastrophe of public suspicion of adulteration of pet food and you can imagine how ready your husband will be to come to terms.'

Julia had sat upright and clasped one knee. She now leaned further forward. She stared, frowning.

'You really mean all this, don't you. You're serious about it.'

Surprise, pain, reproach flitted in turn across his face. 'My dear Julia!' The centre of the little pink mouth suddenly tightened in a mischievous smirk. 'I am nothing if not an honourable man. I am contracted to help you. Had you doubted it?'

She had turned her gaze elsewhere, thinking, not listening. A finger was raised. She touched her lip, smiled. 'You asked, didn't you, on which night it would be convenient to be done away with . . .'

'Fatuously put. I'm sorry.'

'No, no. Please don't be. This really could be a lovely idea.'

'Actually, before you . . .'

'Hey, do you think they'll keep him in a cell all night?' Julia was hugging her knees, eyes sparkling. 'God, he'd hate that. And if they get a search warrant they'll find his precious collection of girlie magazines. Hey, I'd love to see a couple of Flaxborough bobbies trying to puzzle out that dreadful rubber thing he sent away to Liverpool for.'

Mr Rothermere raised his hand. 'My dear, you will have leisure shortly in which to picture Mr Harton's discomfiture. We have in mind for you an exceedingly pleasant little retreat on the Norfolk coast. What are your feelings about that?'

She shrugged, her head a little on one side, but made no reply.

'This I promise you: the food there is . . .' He joined middle finger and thumb to signify indescribable excellence, and kissed the air.

How continental, thought Julia. She said: 'All right, suppose I disappear. What next?'

'Nothing for a while. Two, perhaps three days. Your husband will be uneasy, but I think he will not do anything. This lapse will look bad later, if and when the police begin making inquiries. At the end of three days, we shall make a preliminary approach. He will be told that if he does not agree to a reasonable divorce settlement at the figure my organisation suggests – twenty thousand pounds – your anxious friends and relatives will report your sudden and unexplained absence to the authorities.'

'To which, knowing David, I suspect he will say: go ahead and sod your eyes and much good may it do you. He does tend to be truculent when asked for money.'

'Ah, but our inquiries show that he is also shrewd in assessing odds. If I may say so, Julia, you have lived with him at too close quarters to have seen anything but rapaciousness and arrogance. He knows the score, this fellow; we don't have to worry about that.'

'So?'

'So he will see certain possibilities and he will not like them. He will agree to pay.'

She remained a while in thought. Then she said: 'One thing I'd rather like to know. Why is he supposed to have murdered me? You must grant even David the intelligence to see that the police won't take a motiveless killing very seriously.'

Mr Rothermere smiled. 'You do yourself less than justice, Julia. Jealousy – what else? The discovery that so beautiful a woman has a secret lover would drive any husband to homicide, I assure you.'

'There's one small snag, darling. A secret lover is just what I don't happen to have. Or are you volunteering?'

'You really are sweet.' He glanced at his watch. 'And it's true that I don't have another engagement until five-thirty. Let us, however, first have regard to the – how shall I say? – the practicalities of the problem.'

Seeing him get up from his chair, Julia pulled straight her skirt but remained on the divan. She eyed him with something of provocative speculation.

Mr Rothermere did not look at her. He went into the bathroom and returned with a tubular metal stand, about six feet high when he extended it fully. To this he clamped the camera. He placed the stand between the window and the divan and spent a few moments adjusting the camera mounting. He peered through the viewfinder, squinted round it at Julia and altered a couple of lens settings. Every movement he made had a balletic nicety that contrasted oddly with the shortness and plumpness of his legs, which Julia's position enabled her to notice for the first time.

'What the hell are you doing?' she asked, not unamiably.

He gazed at her through the frame of his fingers. 'You know, you have quite a bit of' – he turned and did something infinitely precise to the shutter control – 'Ingrid about you. Strictly professional' – the finger frame again – 'but once off the set, very companionable, very civilised.'

'Ingrid?'

In sudden dismay, Mr Rothermere struck his brow. 'God, your Madeira! My manners are really quite appalling.' From the bureau he produced a squat, very dark bottle and two plain tumblers. 'And they would seem to be matched by the establishment's drinking ware. I'm sorry.'

He more than half-filled each glass. She accepted hers and sipped. This was a much sweeter and, she thought, more flavoursome wine than the one in the restaurant.

'Nice,' she said.

He looked pleased to hear it.

'My husband has nothing but whisky at home. He doesn't like it much, but he knows I can't stand it, so he lashes it down quite bravely. It seems to help him raise his unpleasantness level.'

Mr Rothermere regarded her thoughtfully for a while. 'You could have done better for yourself, I suppose.'

'By Christ! The understatement of this and every other year!' She emptied her glass at one swig. Her skirt had ridden up again. Disregarding it, she hunched forward, cheek on knee, and stared blankly at the window.

'Not that I am confident,' said Mr Rothermere, 'that the lover we have selected for you would have been a notable improvement.'

She raised her head. 'I'm not with you, darling.'

'Of course not. But I am about to explain.' He affected not to have noticed her empty glass. 'We agreed – and it is perfectly obvious – that your husband must be credited with a powerful and, if possible, demonstrable reason for ending your sweet life. Correct? So. So a lover has to be provided. Policemen, remember, are middle-class moralists to a man; in their book, cuckoldry and burglary are equally heinous. But whom do we appoint? It must be someone who will cooperate, someone sexually vigorous and preferably free of responsibilities, someone, if possible, who cannot be too closely investigated. You can imagine our difficulty.'

Julia, who had been attending with mournful intensity, slowly shook her head.

'But then,' announced Mr Rothermere, 'quite suddenly and out of the blue – the perfect candidate.' With the air of a conjuror, he picked up the cutting Julia had seen him take from the drawer. He handed it to her.

A little blearily, Julia read. She looked up. 'I don't get it.'

'Your secret paramour. Mr Robert Digby Tring!'

Mr Rothermere was looking his most benign. She heard a curious sound. The man from Happy Endings Inc. was emitting a nasal hum of satisfaction; at that moment he looked like a big bearded bee.

'But he's dead, according to this.'

The bee stopped humming. 'Exactly. Wasn't it your uncontrollable grief at his demise that gave the game away and brought on your head a husband's jealous fury?'

Gradually the bewilderment left Julia's face. She looked first thoughtful, then mildly amused. Delight dawned. 'Hey, this is bloody marvellous!'

'I thought it might appeal to you.' Mr Rothermere had opened a closet door and was pulling out a big suitcase.

'Poor David will never survive the social slur. His missus having it off with a Hell's Angel. And one of the Trings, at that.' Julia stretched precariously and possessed herself of the Madeira. 'Know the Terrible Trings, do you? Ooo, Mortimer ...' She attempted to whistle, gave up, and concentrated on getting the cork out of the bottle. 'Actually ...' She paused, then repeated with great deliberation 'Ac-tu-ally ...'

'Yes?'

'Actu-ally I wouldn't have minded. David's a great lad for showing off his hose but he couldn't put a real fire out to save his life.'

Mr Rothermere looked sympathetic and murmured something about sexual behavourism and a conversation he once had had with a man called Jung. Julia thought he sounded very reassuring. She lay flat on the divan, closed her eyes, executed a brief hula movement with her pelvis and made a 'rrrhummm' noise in imitation of a motor-cycle engine. She looked happy but hungry.

He took the bottle from her hand, carefully poured her a small drink, and passed it to her. 'I suggest, my love, that before we grow too convivial we get the photography done. Have I your cooperation?'

Julia looked up at the camera on its stand and gave it a wink. She bared one shoulder and struck an attitude in a parody of seductive guile.

'Yes, but I think we shall need something a little more intense, a fraction more . . .' He shrugged, his hands open as if offering gifts.

'Obscene?'

A hand rose at once. 'No, oh dear, no. Nothing actually indecent. I fancy the right phrase would be artistically provocative. All right? Picasso, I remember, used to ask me occasionally to arrange a model for him because he said sex was music and it needed a musician to read the score, not a painter. He was an astonishingly modest man, that fellow.'

Mr Rothermere opened the suitcase. Julia turned on her stomach in order to peep over the side of the divan. She saw that the case contained a full set of motor-cycle leathers and a bright orange crash helmet.

Mr Rothermere held the helmet aloft. It bore a black stencilled representation of a winged skull.

'May I suggest,' he said, 'this' – he laid the helmet beside her – 'and these' – a pair of black leather gauntlets with silver studs across the knuckles came from the case – 'and these, so long as they fit, which I devoutly trust.'

Julia examined his third offering: knee boots in soft black leather-imitating plastic. She compared one of their soles with her own shoe. 'Should do.' Without looking at him, she reached up as if in expectation of further articles.

Mr Rothermere snapped the case shut. She turned and stared at it stupidly, swaying a little.

He took off his jacket, hung it meticulously on a chair back, and began unknotting his tie. He spoke to her over his shoulder.

'I would have suggested your changing in the bathroom,

but I know you are too honest, too live, a person to suffer from bourgeois susceptibilities.'

She surveyed in silence for a few seconds the boots, gloves and helmet, then suddenly giggled.

'My soon-to-be-late-I-hope husband is a waffle addict.'

'I beg your pardon?'

'You talk about bour ... bourgeois whatsits. Guess what David and his Bobby-May get up to. Oh, yes, one of his more amiable habits is to describe to me how Miss Lintz turns him on, as he puts it.'

'Yes, but waffles ...'

'Oh, that – well, it seems to involve her sitting on a couple of tennis racquets for ten minutes. Butter comes into it somewhere as well, for God's sake.'

'Cultox,' observed Mr Rothermere, 'manufacture eighty-two per cent of the world's margarine. Think of that.'

Kicking off one shoe, she drew on a boot and lay on her back, the leg on erect display. It was, Mr Rothermere noted, a singularly shapely leg. She stroked from knee to thigh. 'God, wouldn't David just love this! He's kinky as all get out, poor bastard.'

He glanced at the poised camera, then at Julia once more. 'Don't forget you still have tights on.' It was the quiet, unemotional observation of a photographer rather than a seducer.

Mr Rothermere came and stood over her. 'Passion without practicality can be self-defeating. Here – let me ...'

She closed her eyes, at the same time raising her hips slightly. Gently he peeled towards himself the nylon second skin, bent over, kissed very lightly the gold-downed flesh. Julia's blind smile was annihilated instantly by her sharp intake of breath.

'I think,' said Mr Rothermere, in a tone of murmurous admiration that was almost entirely genuine, 'that I have not seen so attractive a woman for a very long time.'

Julia half-opened one eye. 'How long?'

He gave her chin a brief, playful caress. 'Since 1956.' The

hand passed down the line of her throat, gentle but confident, and curved about her breast. 'No, I tell a lie. 1949. In Istanbul.'

She felt cool air invade shoulders, then breasts, and caught herself breathing so rapidly that her mouth was drying, so she closed her lips tight, but almost at once the word 'yes' broke through and she went on helplessly repeating it in a series of gasps until the movement of hands over and beneath her had ceased and the cool air was on her whole body, but only for a tiny while until warmth, intense, heavy, possessive, enveloped her. She gave a great sigh and opened her eyes. She was looking straight into the lens of the camera above. There echoed ridiculously in her head the command given at some school photograph ritual. 'Say Cheese.' But only for an instant.

Not that it mattered. Mr Rothermere, quite unprofessionally moved by the occasion, had not had the heart to set the delayed shutter release.

He retrieved the situation half an hour later, with all the props in place and with a degree of eager cooperation on Julia's part that persuaded him to the happy conclusion that the day's work had made him a friend.

Chapter Seven

GRANDMA TRING STOOD SQUARE ON HER STOCKY OLD legs in Flaxborough Market Place and stared up at the gyrating modules of Space Shot. Her face was brown and wondrously wrinkled, with a shrewd, sucked-in mouth, a nose much punished by a lifetime of reckless inquiry and assertion, and a chin like a sea captain's. Lending shade to her eyes, quick and black as rain beetles, was the last surviving example of what had been standard headgear among the older women of the harbour district when Grandma Tring was born there eighty-two years ago – a man's flat cloth cap.

For a while, she watched the coloured cars climb, dip and revolve, and listened to the whoops and squeals of their more excited passengers. Then she turned, spat, and trundled off through the fair towards East Street.

Grandma Tring paid scant attention to the rest of the huge mechanical contrivances that now dominated Flaxborough Fair. They seemed to her to offer ordeals rather than enjoyment. What had happened to the Golden Horses, the great shining prancers, with red nostrils flaring like Charlie Dugbine's used to do when she let him take her round the back of the hut beside the Field Street level crossing, and all the little flags flying on the top, and the painted pictures of cowboys and Neptune and Roman chariots, and the twisty brass rails going up and down with the horses, and the boom and blare and ting-a-ling of the steam organ as you went round past it and saw the ginger-bread stall again and then the Try-your-Strength with its gong in the sky, and then the girls from the seed warehouse, waving, and up came the steam organ once again and a fleeting chance to see all the bits of mirror on it and the wonderfully painted model musicians working like mad to thump drums and ring bells? Where were the stately Twin Yachts, hanging magically in mid-air for a moment before swinging past each other and up again with a gentlemanly little double cough of steam? And how, for heaven's sake, did young men nowadays put their girls in an itching and asking when there were no swingboats to stand up in and bunch their muscles while they heaved on ropes like blue and scarlet catkins until the girls screamed for them to stop but not really wanting them to because it was so exciting to see Saint Laurence's tower keep turning upside down and to know that the lads on the coconut shies were looking up their flying skirts?

As soon as she could push her way through the crowd at the north end of the Market Place, Grandma Tring escaped through a side street into the relative quiet of Priory Lane and thence stumped along to Fen Street.

Despite the Tring family's long history of conflict with authority, its matriarchal head had no qualms about entering a police station. On the contrary, she seemed to feel that as regular customers, so to speak, of the law, she and hers were entitled to some privilege in the matter of invoking it.

She ignored the inquiries hatch and went up to the counter behind which Police Constable Braine was doing some pencil-chewing.

She rapped on the counter. Braine took the pencil out of his mouth and scowled. He looked like a bespectacled toad.

'I want to see the head lad,' announced Grandma Tring.

'You want to what?'

'Come on, duck. Git off yer arse. I want the bean pole with the yeller hair. The inspector. And nobody else. Not that wet bloody errand boy of his, neither.'

Constable Braine's fury at being called 'duck' by this unseemly old besom was ameliorated somewhat by the salty disrespect offered Sergeant Love, whose equable disposition was in Braine's opinion a most unpolicemanly failing.

'Name?' He reached grudgingly for the telephone.

A disdainful silence.

'Mrs Tring, is it?'

The old woman's back stiffened. She wagged a bony finger. 'Don't you play silly buggers with me, son.'

Braine pressed a key on the switchboard. 'Miss Tring is here, sir. She'd like to see you if it's convenient.'

To Braine's deep disgust, Inspector Purbright not only agreed to see Grandma Tring at once, but asked that she be made comfortable in an adjoining room in order to be saved a climb upstairs. Most galling of all was the instruction to get her a cup of tea if she wanted one.

The old woman followed her reluctant guide and tested all the chairs in the room before settling into the largest and least dilapidated. Braine watched gloomily from the doorway. At a moment when her inquisitive gaze was directed at a spot safely remote from himself, he mouth-mimed the question 'Tea?' (*Of course I asked her, sir – she ignored me.*)

'Yiss,' snapped Grandma Tring, to Braine's surprise and alarm. He stared at the back of her head and fancied for an instant that he saw supplementary eyes, but they were only the glass heads of her hat pins.

'And plenty of sugar, mind,' she added.

Inspector Purbright found the old woman contentedly nosing the steam from a canteen mug. He told her it was a shame about young Digger, and he was sorry.

She accepted his sympathy without remark, but seemed to pass it as genuine. Rocking gently over her tea, she asked when that dratted trial was going to be got over because it wasn't doing any good to anybody.

'It's an inquest, Miss Tring, not a trial. The coroner asks questions and tries to find out what caused the accident.'

'That was nivver no bloody accident, son. You can have twenty inquests and they wain't make it any different. Inquests isn't nobbut wind and piss.'

Purbright appeared to consider this axiom carefully. Then he asked:

'Miss Tring, have you any reason for supposing that your grandson's death was other than accidental?'

She gave a businesslike grunt and leaned forward.

'Reasons? Listen, I could give you reasons enough to boil three and bust six, but you ain't got all day no more than I have, so shut up and pay heed. It weren't accidental because it were on purpose. That's the first thing you nivver got told, ain't it. And here's another. There was them after 'im as he knew something about and likely wanted a quid or two for, as is natural in a lad.'

'Ah, now that I did not know.' The inspector nodded sapiently.

Grandma Tring paused to suck up some tea. Her face saddened. 'We reckoned at home,' she said, 'that young Digger had got into bad company.'

The possibility of their existing within a hundred miles of Flaxborough any company susceptible of unfavourable comparison with the Trings had never occurred to Purbright.

The old woman, supposing his startled expression to indicate concern, elaborated.

'What kind o' company? Fancy company. That's what kind. And fancy's bad as often as not. We reckoned Digger was sarvin' wimmin out of 'is class.'

'Sarving?'

She peered at him, dubiously. 'Aye, sarvin' – like 'orses an' 'ogs. Ain't you nivver sarved yer missus?'

He led her back to the point at issue. With what lady, or ladies, had her grandson formed a misalliance?

Ah, she couldn't help him there – not as to names. Digger and his friends didn't use names. The girls they picked up were too busy getting pleasured by one lad or another in the old bike shed to be called anything special. Well, when you were young, you didn't bother. But there was one tottie she'd seen him with in town, not just once neither, though at a distance, and that one she could tell right away was the scent and pink frock kind. *And* she'd got a motor of her own.

'A married woman, would you say, Miss Tring?' Purbright asked.

'Shouldn't wonder. Them's the ones as touch up easiest. Specially after church.' Grandma Tring's sudden cackle made the inspector jump. He recalled, and did not disbelieve, Sergeant Bill Malley's assertion that she was frequently the guest occupant, with her knitting, of the big old basket chair in the building behind Edward Crescent that served the Flaxborough Hellcats as motor-cycle store, clubhouse and bordello.

'If you'll forgive my saying so, what you've told me up to now doesn't add up to very much,' Purbright said. 'It can hardly be said to prove that someone wished your grandson harm.'

Grandma Tring scowled. 'All right, then. What about the photo, eh? That fellow who came round. Said he was from the paper, but he bloody wasn't, 'cause I've asked. And what' – she thrust her face closer – 'about Digger's medal?'

'Medal?'

'Ah, they nivver told you about that, did they?'

'No. I can't say they did. What did he win it for?'

'I an't sayin' 'e won it. Not like in a war or jumpin' in rivers an' that. But 'e'd got it and once 'e showed it me, and 'e said, Gran, 'e said, that little old sod's worth a thousand pounds any day I like to pick up a tellyphone. That's what 'e said. And 'e meant it. A thousand pounds. So where's it gone, eh?'

'How do you know it's gone anywhere?'

'It's not in Digger's things. We've all had a look.'

'Can you describe this medal?' Purbright squatted down by the old woman's side and handed her a pencil and a folded envelope. 'Show me what it looked like.'

She smoothed the paper flat on a thigh skirted in what seemed to be black roofing felt, and made a wavery circle with the pencil.

'Ain't no good at drorin',' she said. A few squiggles and dots appeared within the circle, which was about an inch and a quarter across. 'Them's printing,' explained Grandma Tring. 'Words.'

'Can you remember what they were?'

She shook her head. 'Digger kep' it in 'is 'and. Aye, but I reckon' – an eye half closed in effort of recall – 'as it was somethin' to do with Mister Churchill.'

'Sir Winston Churchill?'

'Yiss. 'Im.'

There was silence while the old woman stared at her sketch and ruminatively twisted the little bunch of hairs that decorated a mole on her jaw. Then the pencil went to work again. Some short jabs and dashes appeared on the rim of the circle.

'It was cut about a bit,' she announced. 'Sort of jaggy.'

Purbright took back pencil and envelope and rose to his feet.

'I'll certainly let you know if it turns up, Miss Tring. But there is something else missing, isn't there? A framed picture of your gra . . .'

'Silver.' The word snipped off the tail of his sentence like a sprung mousetrap.

'My sergeant tells me that the man to whom you handed that photograph – and frame – told you he was from the *Flaxborough Citizen* office. You now know that wasn't true.'

She pursed her lips, as if the only appropriate comment was too venomous to be let out.

'I understand from Mr Love that he was a bearded man, smartly dressed, well spoken. A biggish man – is that right?'

Yes, that was it, biggish. And with the looks of a fancy eater. A prissy talker, too, as if he had a bit of foreigner in him. She would not be all that surprised if he put scent on his whiskers.

'What sort of questions did he ask you, Miss Tring?'

'Well, about Digger, didn't 'e. Where 'e went to school and if 'e'd played football and such and where 'e went to work. All that. It would've been a lovely piece in the paper after what I told him.'

'And what did you tell him?'

Grandma Tring looked away. 'Oh, this 'n that.' There was a pause. 'About Digger's dad gettin' the Victoria Cross, and the time Digger saved the dog meat factory from burnin' down, and about doctors that measured up 'is brain when 'e was four and sayin' 'e'd got enough for a vicar an' a librarian both at one go. Fam'ly things. Jus' fam'ly.'

'Pity he wasn't really from the newspaper,' said Purbright, meaning it.

She snorted. 'The fleechin' bugger! If my lads lay claws on 'im, they'll use 'is eyeballs for bottle stoppers.'

'A short while ago,' said the inspector, when he judged her ire to have subsided, 'you said something to the effect that your grandson possessed information that he thought was worth money. People were "after him" I think you said.'

'I might 've,' she said, warily.

'Have you any idea who they were, these people?'

No, she hadn't. God rest his soul, Digger had been a close young sod.

'In that case,' said Purbright, 'I suppose you'll not be able to tell me what the information was that he considered valuable.'

He supposed right. Unless . . .

'Yes?'

Unless, the old woman said after deliberation, it had something to do with tombstones. She looked up. 'R.I.P. – that's what they put on tombstones, ain't it?'

Purbright nodded, and she went on:

'Aye, well, I asked 'im what 'e thought 'e was up to with 'is medals and 'is tellyphones and 'is tales about knowin' this an' that and the other, and what does 'e do but wink his poor little good eye at his Gran and thump the side of his nose with his finger like that and say "R.I.P." I says, What? And again 'e says "R.I.P." And looks pleased as if 'e's farted in church. But that's all I could get out of 'im, and now 'e's gone, poor lad.'

The inspector suggested that Digger had merely intended to reprove her inquisitiveness with a tactfully oblique reference. Had he wanted the matter to be allowed to 'rest in peace' in fact?

Grandma Tring scowled dubiously. No, it was that missing medal as she reckoned was at the bottom of it all. A thousand pound was a rare old lot of money to be got by telephone, even in these wicked times. And Digger wasn't a lad as would lie to his Gran.

Purbright later took up the point with Sergeant Love.

Love confirmed that none of the younger Trings would dare employ at home those imaginative gifts for which they were noted elsewhere.

'In that case, unless the old woman fed me the story for some obscure purpose of her own, we can assume that this medal, or whatever it is, does exist.'

Love thought about that. 'There's no medal on the missing property list.'

'No? Well, in any case I can't see one fetching any extravagant sum of money, not even for sentimental reasons.'

'Could be blackmail,' suggested the sergeant, incurably optimistic in the matter of High Crime.

'I've yet to hear of anybody ready to pay lest the neighbours get to know he's a hero. Incidentally, since when has Digger's father been a V.C.?'

'Since when has Digger had a father?'

Purbright knew better than to suspect a witticism. Love was by no means a solemn young man, but he was an essentially serious one. The truth about the Trings was that they had genetic peculiarities similar to those of the hive, in as much as all the fertilising was done by casual, drone-like suitors who were soon driven away again by matriarchal tyranny.

'Perhaps,' said the inspector, 'the old woman's obvious preoccupation with medals has led us up the garden a bit. She didn't examine the thing closely. It could have been something of high intrinsic value that just *looked* like a medal.'

'Such as?'

'A slug of platinum, say. Cast in a form that can be called artistic to get round the metal-hoarding regulations.'

Love frowned. 'Who'd want to hoard platinum?'

'There are those, Sid, whose gains are so considerable and so ill-gotten that they can't wait to transmute them into some thing respectable. I believe the Americans call it "laundering". Do you suppose there is such a thing as a Churchill Medallion?'

'Probably. There are Churchill tanks and Churchill cigars and no end of Churchill Avenues.'

Purbright shook his head vaguely. 'Just something else Grandma said.'

'Was she on about that photograph again?'

'She was.'

'Fancy Digger having his picture taken.' Love looked almost wistful. 'One without a number on it, I mean. They reckon he had a tottie though, so it might have been for her.'

'The old woman spoke of a girl friend – one complete with scent and her own motor car, according to Grandma. Would that not have been out of character?'

Love considered, then suddenly brightened. 'Perhaps,' he said, 'Digger was a rich woman's plaything.'

'Perhaps,' murmured the inspector. He looked pained.

A moment later he remembered something else that Grandma Tring had said. About her grandson's 'good eye'.

'Digger wasn't blind in one eye, was he, Sid?'

'No, not blind. He came off his bike about two years ago, though, and messed one side of his face up a bit. It left a biggish scar under one eye.' Love pointed to his own unblemished cheek in illustration.

'Ah, yes,' said Purbright. 'I noticed that when they collected him.'

Chapter Eight

THE FOLLOWING MORNING WAS THURSDAY. MRS Cutlock did not come to work for the Hartons on Thursdays. Thornton had been taken off to his boarding school in Yorkshire the previous day by Julia's father. David Harton, who was required by the Cultox 'My Pal My Boss' code to remain in his office late enough on one evening a week to be available to discuss night shift problems, was now, at half past ten, on his way to the Doggigrub plant. Julia waited a further quarter of an hour, then began to pack a large suitcase.

The task was unexpectedly difficult. There were many clothes from which to choose. Yet again and again a dress or coat or pair of slacks went into the case only to be reconsidered, sighed over, and thrust back. One had to look decent, even in retreat; but any suggestion of deliberate emigration would be dangerous.

One thing was sure. David would not have the slightest idea of what she had taken. He never noticed what she wore and took no interest in her shopping – beyond deploring the fact that it cost money. He certainly would be without a clue when it came to giving the police an inventory.

When? She frowned, suddenly anxious. *If* it came to that, she had meant. But no, surely to God he wouldn't prove that bloody stubborn and stupid. Not when his own neck was threatened, he wouldn't.

She retrieved from the case a dress in brilliant orange jersey, hung it back in the wardrobe and selected instead an outfit in autumnal beige. No point in looking conspicuous, even though the game wasn't going to be allowed to get to a really absurd stage, like a police hunt or something.

Shoes. A pair for looks, a pair for walking. September walks in Norfolk. Very pleasant. She must remember to impress on Mortimer the need to let her know if things threatened to go too far. There was Thornton to be considered. Though her father was sure to have had him in mind when he called in Mortimer Rothermere's organisation in the first place.

Julia smiled when she remembered the inscrutability maintained by her father while he marshalled the child into his car yesterday and prepared to drive off to Yorkshire. No wonder the boys at his school called him Clam. He'd let all her hints go by, not even rising to the bait when she'd wished the trip 'happy ending'.

At a quarter to twelve, she carried the packed case through the door that led from the kitchen into the back of the garage.

She put the case into the boot of her own small car. The garage could not be seen from the road, nor was it overlooked by the window of any other house. She watched the drive carefully just the same until the case had been stowed and the boot lid pressed shut. A sense of elation was beginning to take hold of her. It heightened her consciousness, both of self and of relevant externals. This, she supposed, was what people addicted to dangerous games meant when they claimed to be having 'fun'. Well, so it was.

Julia drove into town the long way round, up Partney Drive into Hunting's Lane, then down past the park and through Fen Street. The late Victorian washhouse-gothic home of Flaxborough's police force in Fen Street, she seemed to be seeing for the first time. It looked huge and fortress-like. Two men in uniform were emerging ponderously from a side door. Julia looked quickly away and kept her face averted until she reached the East Street junction where she turned right and joined the trail of traffic waiting to squeeze past the booths and rides in the crowded Market Place ahead.

The town bridge, too, was congested, but after the left turn into Burton Place the west-bound traffic became sparse. In another five minutes the little blue car had travelled the length of Burton Lane and was entering the grounds of the motel just beyond the Oxby Moor crossroads.

Julia drove to the back of the reception building where there was a crudely paved parking area. It contained only three cars. One of them, a big yellow saloon, was standing at the far side of the space, half concealed by bushes that had straggled through gaps in the tall boundary fence.

There was no attendant. A notice board warned of the management's accepting no responsibility for something or other. Julia gave it no more than a glance. She drove across the area and made a reverse turn into position alongside the yellow car.

She got out. The car was Rothermere's. His *Times* of two days before still lay on the back seat. It and the missing winder handle on the passenger side gave her a sense of familiarity.

The boot of the Fiat opened easily. Inside was a parcel, a bulky parcel securely but inexpertly tied with thick string. It was heavy and awkward enough to need a two-armed effort to lift.

Less than a minute later, Julia was driving back along Burton Lane. Her slight breathlessness was not the result of switching case and parcel in accordance with Rothermere's instructions. It arose from sheer excitement, from a mounting persuasion that these curious things she was steeling herself to perform – things she always had supposed peculiar to the fantasy world of the thriller – were not only well within her capacity but were actually going to prove effective.

On her return trip through Fen Street, she stared boldly at the police station. A tall man with corn-coloured hair, hatless, was standing outside in leisurely conversation. An inspector, she thought, remembering having seen him with her father on some school occasion. The tall man, endowed perhaps with a policeman-like sensitivity to stares, glanced at her as she passed. He smiled shyly.

When she reached home again, Julia was surprised to see the time was only 12.20. It was going to be a damned long afternoon. She cleared the breakfast table and washed up. Slowly and methodically, she put away the china and cutlery.

She considered lunch. Not yet. A sherry might be a better idea. Appetite did not respond. She had a second sherry, drinking it more slowly. At one o'clock, she switched on the portable radio in the kitchen and listened with half consciousness to the news while she viewed the small reserve of convenience foods from which she occasionally drew a meal when she was on her own.

A four-ounce portion of a compound labelled, incredibly, 'Ham'n'Egg-Burger' was the only alternative to the extreme gastronomic polarity of baked beans and truffled oysters. She offered it, albeit with misgivings, to the can opener.

The telephone rang.

'Julia?' It was David, of course. Why the hell did he always sound like this on the phone, as though he expected some other woman to be in charge of the house?

'Naturally.'

'Nothing natural about it. You could be one of a thousand people. Surely a simple announcement of identity wouldn't cripple you.' (*God! – argue, argue, argue . . .*)

'What is it you want?'

'I'd like you to fetch me tonight. The bloody car's broken down.'

Oh, god, now what. Today of all days. 'Broken down?' She tried to think quickly of ways in which her strategy might be threatened.

'Look, I don't have time to give you a run-down on all failure factors relevant to the internal combustion engine. Just accept that the car won't go, right? Daddy's motor broken. Wheels not go round. Mummy come at half-past seven, yes? Half seven.'

He rang off. Slowly Julia replaced the receiver. She returned to the kitchen and did some more thinking while she unlidded the 'Ham'n'Egg-Burger' and sliced it into a frying pan. By the time it was emitting its promised sizzle of true country goodness, she realised that, far from upsetting the day's plan, the car incident might almost be an improvement. Her presence in the factory at the day's end would not now need to seem fortuitous; it was David who would be seen to have engineered it.

After lunch, Julia brought in from the garage the parcel for which she had exchanged her case of clothing. She cut the string and opened out the single sheet of brown wrapping paper.

She stared dreamily for some seconds at the black zip-fronted tunic, the breeches in the same soft, leather-textured plastic, and the boots, supple and with heightened heels. Then she drew on a pair of pink rubber housework gloves and, carrying one of the boots, crossed the hall into the sitting-room.

A shoe was lying in the fireplace, another on the seat of a chair. She measured it, sole to sole, against the boot. They matched, as she had known they would. David had unnaturally small feet for a man. They and his tiny, yet clumsy, hands seemed as if they had ceased growing when he was about ten.

His head appeared small, too, but she could not be sure about that. He never wore a hat, and because he was sensitive about a tendency to premature greying he kept his hair cut very short. So there was no helmet in the parcel, Mortimer having agreed that a bad guess might spoil the whole thing.

Back in the kitchen, Julia spread boots, tunic and breeches on a clear section of bench and with a slightly waxed cloth systematically rubbed the entire plasticised area and every button and piece of metal that might have retained finger-prints. She did not find the task in the least onerous: it was more like the first intriguing and satisfying trial in practice of some process learned on an arts and crafts course.

Still wearing gloves, she bundled the gear together with deliberate awkwardness and re-wrapped them in newspaper. She viewed the resulting package, and nodded, satisfied. An authentic Harton creation. She stuffed it into a floor level recess beneath the sink and pushed it as far back as it would go.

There remained the original paper and string. She could not remember if Mortimer had said anything about them. Never mind, she was capable of thinking for herself and of being thorough. She carried the wrappings to a corner of the garden where there was a wire basket which David, in a brief flirtation with horticulture, once had bought for the burning of fallen leaves. She made in it a bonfire of the paper and a couple of armfuls of the early sheddings of a big chestnut tree.

It was not yet half-past two. She tried to relax and listen to an orchestral concert on radio but gave up after a quarter of an hour.

Setting off to fetch a book from upstairs, she found herself wandering from room to room as if making an inventory of their contents and committing to memory the exact arrangement of furniture.

It was ridiculous, this restlessness. She was behaving like a nervous middle-aged woman embarking on her first shop-lifting expedition. There was nothing criminal in what she was doing. Nobody was going to cross-examine her. She had every justification for what she intended – to frighten a self-centred, brutish husband and to force him into making amends for his treatment of her.

Perhaps, Julia reasoned, a bath would help. At least it would pass some time.

She ran water to a slightly greater depth than usual, but made it a little cooler; it needed to be calming but not soporific.

Tossed among a mixture of toothbrushes, paste tubes, and razor and blades at the back of the wash basin bench was an unstoppered bottle, the latest addition, Julia supposed, to David's assiduous gleanings from the field of male cosmetics. She picked it up. 'Forestry Balm, a Skin-Toning Compound of Twenty-nine Costly Herbs from Finland.' She sent a couple of glugs into the bath water. They fizzed briefly, then spread in green whorls. There arose a steamy, obtrusive perfume. It reminded Julia of the smell of breath-sweeteners, whose use had been one of her husband's earliest essays in the achievement of sexual irresistibility.

She undressed in the bedroom. The bruises on both legs that testified to the kicks David had delivered two days before were now starkly defined, their colour yellowish like tobacco stains. Julia stared at them for a long while in the mirror, her face showing no emotion save perhaps thoughtfulness, satisfaction even.

She turned away at last and moved about the room, lazily casual. At the window, she paused to look out upon the rowan trees, scarlet clustered, and the closely set beeches that formed now a flame-coloured wall of leaf guarding the privacy of the house and garden. Gently, she pressed her body against the glass. The chill tingled into her breasts and belly. She closed her eyes. Was this how it felt to be a nude painting? David would probably have preferred her to be a big erotic picture. He was great on peeping; had a special face to wear for it – his tolerant, I'll-go-along-with-it intellectual face, that he kept for strip shows at the Masonic.

Julia opened her eyes again to look at the trees and sky. Slowly, almost reluctantly, she drew away from the window, as from an embrace. She left the room and went slowly downstairs.

For five minutes or more, she wandered in and out of rooms. She had never before been naked in any of them. It was marvellous, this solitude, this freedom. And it was only a symbolic foretaste, after all. Soon she would be able to go where she liked, to do what she fancied, when she fancied. To the tune of twenty thousand pounds.

She ascended the stairs like a nude priestess and slid, tongue-tip in ecstatic communion with upper lip, into the green-tinged, gently steaming water.

The weather, which had been bright and warm during most of the day, grew more dull as the afternoon passed. At six o'clock some of the street lamps came on. Julia, making herself a pot of tea, saw the light from one of them through the trees, faint and red like a paper lantern. She frowned; fog would be an unwanted complication.

She drank her tea quickly and without enjoyment. Resisting a chronic inclination to check every room again to ensure that everything indicated a natural and unplanned departure, she left the house at ten minutes past six.

The Doggigrub plant lay on the northern outskirts of Flaxborough. It was set back from the Chalmsbury road, fenced within its own grounds. Broad concrete carriageways circled the factory buildings, some of which were linked by conveyors, big pipes slung overhead like aerial arteries. By the time Julia drove past the gate office and made her way towards the administrative block, most of the daytime production had ceased. A couple of trucks were being loaded with cases in the floodlit transport bay. Plumes of steam marked where a continuous sterilisation plant had been left on automatic setting until morning.

She listened to noises which, though ordinary enough in daylight, were strangely difficult to identify in the gathering dusk; the rolling of an empty can; a chain passing over a pulley; the clash of elevator gates.

Julia had been seen, recognised and respectfully greeted by the gatekeeper. No doubt he had conscientiously set down in his record of traffic the arrival at 18.29 hours of the wife of Doggigrub's chairman and managing director. Still, it would do no harm to have a few more witnesses.

She left the car opposite the main entrance to Administration and walked back to the long, single-storeyed building that housed the dog food processing department.

A pair of men in Doggigrub green overalls were pushing a big scraper back and forth across an area of floor that had acquired a pinkish grey crust. They were the sole occupants of the building.

'Hi,' said Julia, from the doorway.

The men stopped pushing and looked towards her.

'Evening, Mrs Harton,' said the older. His companion nodded nervously. They waited.

'My husband promised me a bit of sight-seeing. He's not about, though, is he?' She tried to grin cheerfully but it wasn't easy. A familiar but loathed smell was beginning to insinuate itself through the masking deodoriser that was constantly being injected into the air supply. It was the unconquerable stink of carrion.

Promptly and eagerly, the men peered about, across, up and down. No, they admitted, Mr Harton was not about.

'Not to worry.' She gave them a nice smile and withdrew.

The younger man said to the older: 'I'd rather be up her than up in Newcastle.' The older man jerked his head in indication of the shadowy shapes of machinery. 'Sight-seeing? Bloody hell!'

Julia returned to where she had left her car. All the lights in the office block were on, although most of the staff had gone home an hour ago. Through one window she saw a pair of women in pinafores and dust caps. They were vigorously up-ending waste paper bins and lashing desk tops with dusters.

A row of three windows belonged to the boardroom. It, too, was lighted, but the curtains of blue and gold striped satin had been drawn. That was where David would be now, with McGregor probably, and Donaldson, and perhaps chinless Higgins, punishing the pink gin and replaying games of golf.

Julia passed into the reception lobby. A girl was seated behind a desk that consisted substantially of a sheet of black glass. She had a phone beside her, but nothing else. Julia thought how sad she looked, as though she had been kept behind after school for something she hadn't done.

'Oh dear, I'm afraid he's in conference,' the girl said, suddenly attentive but looking more pained than ever. She extended a timorous hand towards the phone. 'Would you like me to tell him you're here?'

'No, that's all right, Eileen. I'm a bit early, actually. He *is* expecting me. I'll come back.'

Along the southern boundary of the site occupied by Doggigrub was a path that once had been a bridleway between Northgate and farms on Heston Down. It now was little used and some stretches had become overgrown, but it did not require much diligence, even on a dark evening, to follow this path as far as the opening in the perimeter fence that had been made some years before by dwellers in adjoining Twilight

Close and since renewed by them so perseveringly after each repair that the factory management had finally conceded victory. What the management had not done was to solve the mystery of why the inmates of a local authority's home for the aged should want to have access to the grounds of a pet food manufactory. Many suggestions, some sinister, had been offered. All were wide of the truth, which was simply that the pleasantly landscaped and planted area provided for a few at a time of the old men and women a secluded refuge from the strictures and (much worse) solicitous jollities of their captors.

Julia reached the gap in the fence without having seen anybody or encountered worse obstacles than a patch of thistles and a number of elder bushes whose berries, hanging in shadow at face height, had brushed unexpectedly across her cheeks like bunches of little clammy finger ends.

She climbed through into the driveway of Twilight Close and walked swiftly and as quietly as she could to the rear exit, which was used only by tradesmen making deliveries to the kitchens during the day.

The big yellow Fiat was waiting on the opposite side of Leicester Avenue, twenty yards down.

Julia hurried to the car and got in.

Mr Rothermere, swaddled in warm air, cigar smoke and a Mozart quintet, gave her a sideways beam of welcome.

'No one saw you leave?'

'Not a soul.'

He nodded and squeezed her thigh.

The journey through Lincolnshire and Cambridgeshire into Norfolk took two and a half hours. For some of the time Julia slept, leaning lightly against Mr Rothermere's shoulder. She did not snore, a fact he found curiously endearing; indeed, twice during this interlude he looked down at the sleep-smoothed face with sadness and something that could have been self-reproach.

They stopped in Norwich for a leisurely dinner amidst oak

and stone and pewter and American Express cards. Mr Rothermere played a solo on the wine list with characteristic panache, a performance he followed up by recounting how the Gironde Maquis had sabotaged a consignment of wine for Germany by putting into it corn plasters that fastidious Nazis would suppose to have floated off the feet of the grape treaders.

'One actually did get into a bottle that was delivered to Goering.' He raised a finger, as if admonishing her laughter. 'No, it really did.' Somewhere in those jauntily curled whiskers was a grin, surely? She began, warily; 'Were you ... I mean, I haven't really gathered ...' But always the barrier of modesty. 'God, it was so long ago. And so dreadfully unimportant.' She did not press him. Some of his memories must be pretty terrible.

As soon as Julia climbed wearily out of the car and stood on the empty forecourt of the little Cromer hotel, she was aware of the long breathing of the sea. She was slapped fully awake by the pungency of salt and wet sand and mats of weed. She stared at the dark that hung, like a heavy curtain, beyond the cliff's edge. Such intensity of blackness compelled a straining to discern the slightest pinpoint of light that would make it credible. After a while, Julia saw a tiny gleam, then another, fainter. Ships, she supposed, far out. Then high up, a diamond speck, two, six, a dozen. A glittering frost of stars. Feeling foolishly relieved, she turned and followed her escort into the hotel.

The woman who appeared in response to Mr Rothermere's shaking a little silver handbell at the reception counter was a florid-complexioned, dumpy woman with a round face and beaklike nose that gave her the profile of a parrot. He entered in the register the names of Mʳ and Mrs M. H. Rothermere, Greenfield Lodge, Well Road, Hampstead, London, N.W.3.

'I,' said the parroty lady to Julia, 'am Mrs Cartwright,' and she stared at her with great interest.

'How do you do,' said Julia.

'My wife will be staying on for a few days,' said Mr Rothermere. 'I, alas, must return to town first thing tomorrow. I did mention that in my letter, didn't I?'

Mrs Cartwright inclined her head. 'Mr Cartwright's Army,' she said to Julia. After a pause, the awkwardness of which made Julia wonder if some sort of password was expected of her, she added emphatically: 'Major.' Again there was silence.

Mr Rothermere took charge. Putting an arm round his supposed spouse's shoulder, he leered fondly down at her and said: 'Up the wooden hill you go, little woman. I shouldn't think you'll need much rocking tonight.'

Upon hearing which unpromising sentiment, and not aware from where she stood that it was belied by a hand cupped about Julia's left buttock, Mrs Cartwright turned and sought out the key to their room. At the same time, she hooted two or three times, summoning thereby a stringy, sandy-haired man in khaki shirt and trousers, who took the cases upstairs.

Mr Rothermere followed, with his little woman, a quartern bottle of brandy, two glasses, and the gratitude of Mrs Cartwright for his understanding the problems posed by shortage of staff.

'She does know why I'm here, doesn't she?' Julia demanded anxiously as soon as they were alone.

'But of course.'

'She seemed to be making heavy weather of the Mr and Mrs thing.'

He smiled. 'Your own guilty feelings. Oh, and very nice, too. My analyst maintains that sex without guilt is like Bierwurst without gherkin.'

'When will you be seeing my husband?' Now that the excitement of planning, decision and action was subsiding, Julia felt an emptiness, a bewilderment, that a first brandy was disappointingly slow to dispel.

Mr Rothermere sat beside her on the bed. 'You are going to have to be patient, my dear. He will need to be marinaded a little. At least until after the weekend. The Bureau works to very carefully researched guidelines in these matters. Listen, do you know who is retained as its permanent consultant?'

Julia shook her head. She was conscious of being gently and systematically undressed, but felt for the moment neither resentment nor pleasure.

'Farquharson,' said Mr Rothermere. 'It was to have him handy that they laid the Whitehall–Harley Street hot line in Churchill's day. Amazing man. And yet when I knew him in Vienna – we shared a flat, actually, with a dried yeast salesman, of all things – he was dreadfully shy and stuttered.'

Without interrupting the narrative Mr Rothermere took Julia's glass, drew over the arm thus freed the loop of her brassière, and replaced the glass in her hand.

'This is not generally known, but three prime ministers have gone mad since 1950. Farquharson had them all back on the rails before any serious damage could be done. Except on one occasion, when he was with me, tunny-fishing off Scarborough.' He bent to take off her shoes. 'So you see I too have a guilt complex. I feel personally responsible for Suez.'

Chapter Nine

DAVID HARTON EMERGED FROM THE BOARDROOM OF Northern Nutritionals at five minutes to seven, with Donaldson, his sales director, and two men who had arrived on the London train earlier in the day.

One of these men, although in his early forties, had absolutely white hair, brushed straight back from a broad, baby-pink forehead. The other was sallow of face, a little taller than his companion, and he had a sort of watchful humility that would automatically steer him to the back of any group. Both gave the impression of having extremely small feet and pale, almost bleached, hands. They might have been taken to be investigative emissaries from the Vatican. In fact, they were Cultox men. Central Office of the parent company. Security Division. During the evening, they had accepted one dry sherry apiece.

'Goodnight, gentlemen.' Donaldson peeled off towards his own office to get his coat. He looked unhappy and exhausted.

'Goodnight, Brian.' Harton gave him a condescending, army officer kind of smile.

From reception came Eileen, the late duty girl. 'Oh, Mr Harton . . .'

'Yes, Eileen.' He halted at once, courteous and friendly. Why did the wretched girl always stand and even walk about with her arms folded tightly across her breasts? Petit-bourgeois mock modesty.

'Mrs Harton is here. She said you were expecting her, and not to bother you until you came out.'

'Sure. Sure.' He gave her shoulder a jolly, get-along-home squeeze.

Distantly, a bell rang, signalling the seven o'clock shift. Eileen snatched up scarf and handbag, briefly surveyed her glass desk, and began walking to the door.

Harton frowned suddenly, turned. 'Eileen. . .'

She looked back from the door.

'You say Mrs Harton thinks I'm expecting her?'

'That's right.'

'I'm not, actually. Never mind, though. Where is she now?'

'I don't know. She said she'd be back.'

'Fine.' He waved cheerily. 'Off you go, then.'

The men from Cultox had been looking on, impassively. Now the one with white hair spoke. 'Look. David, you obviously must stay on. If you'll get someone to ring for a taxi, we can easily look after ourselves from now.'

'Nonsense, Charles. We'll do as we arranged. Dinner first, then I'll run you to the station.'

'But your wife . . .'

'Julia does tend to be unpredictable. I'll leave a note on my desk. She may even have gone home.'

They accompanied him to his office. He wrote on his desk pad. *Dining at Roebuck with Charles and Simon – come along if you like.*

The white-haired man was at Harton's shoulder, reading the note. The other, Simon, stood deferentially on the opposite side of the desk. He could read upside down.

'Would our names mean anything to Mrs Harton? Neither of us has ever met her.'

'My dear Charles, does it matter? One tries not to break what good habits one has, such as courtesy and general friendliness – you know? – but the truth is that Julia is, to put it mildly, pretty unrewarding. No, of course your names will mean nothing to her. She'd cut the Archbishops of Canterbury and York if *I* brought them home. I can but hope that the situation will soon be resolved.'

'That, and a certain other situation,' said Simon, piously but with a distinct hint of acerbity. Harton wondered if he had given a sufficiently gratifying emulation of his visitor's way of pronouncing resolved as re*zoal*ved.

'With any luck, one will *evoal*ve from the other,' he said.

Charles puffed his pink, healthy cheeks in good-natured reproof. 'Luck, David? Marketwise, there's no such commodity.' He grinned and patted Harton's arm. 'As you know perfectly well, David. Anyway' – he took a step towards the door, rubbing his hands – 'let us sample the roast beef of old Flaxborough at this marvellous old inn we've heard so much about.'

Harton, who had made no claims concerning either the age or the cuisine of the Roebuck Hotel, both of which were matters of complete indifference to him, was astute enough nevertheless to recognise that a small pit was being dug for his self-esteem.

He determined to take note of the Londoner's technique so that he might use it himself some time.

They left the building by the main door. Julia's car was standing a few yards away. Harton indicated it. 'The wife's. She has a genius for leaving things where they'll be a nuisance. Bless her little heart.'

Simon's smile was understanding.

Just round the corner stood the Hastings-Pumari, in its private port. Charles made himself comfortable in the front passenger seat. Simon entered the back. He stroked the plump suede cushioning. 'Nice,' he said.

The engine fired at once and hummed with perfect manners. Less than ten minutes later, the car drew into the lighted courtyard of the Roebuck.

Charles gazed about him. 'Oh, dear,' he said, pleasantly.

Harton, pausing on his way to the door that led to the dining room, gave him a look of inquiry. Charles pretended to be forcing a brave smile. 'Imagine,' he said, 'the sort of response you'd get if you asked in London for mulled ale!'

They went inside.

Charles examined pointedly the plywood Jacobean panelling that lined the corridor. 'As for genuine roast beef . . .' The enormity of demanding from a London restaurateur this commonplace comestible of Flaxborough he left Harton to picture.

The dining-room was nearly empty. They were shown to a table by the manager, Mr Maddox, who left them with a menu apiece while he went to switch on another couple of lights in honour of the occasion.

'I had rather expected to see a spit,' said Charles, then: 'No, no, old man, I'm only joking. You're right, it's quite a place. Marvellous, David.' He put the menu aside. 'I think I'll have the old English sausage and chips, if I may.'

Harton felt that even his wriest smile would not quite meet

this one. 'Thursday's a bad night,' he offered. 'Staffwise, I mean.'

Charles stared aloft at a ceiling criss-crossed circa 1935 with oak-stained beamwork. He nodded sympathetically.

'Just the same in town, David. But we don't have the compensation of being able to look around and get this marvellous sense of history.'

Mr Maddox served them himself. He was asked by Charles if the sausages were a speciality of the house – made from boar's head, were they? – local herbs? – that sort of thing? To the company, Mr Maddox made grave reply that the recipe was the secret of the hotel's supplier, one of whose ancestors had been tortured to no avail by Cromwellian officers, similarly intrigued. To Mrs Maddox, in the privacy of the kitchen, he announced that some clever dicks from the dog meat factory had been trying to take the piss out of him on account of the Co-op bangers, so instead of making them fresh coffee she could jolly well boil up that lot that had been left over from breakfast.

While sipping which punitive beverage, the Cultox security men broached the matter that had brought them to Flaxborough.

'We had a long talk on the phone yesterday,' said Simon, 'with Rothermere. He is not altogether happy.'

'Oh? That wasn't my impression.'

'When did you last see him, David?' asked Charles.

'Yesterday. There's a little pub up the road at Pennick. I met him there yesterday morning. It's an arrangement we have.'

'He filled you in on progress?'

'Right.'

'Did he express no anxiety at all?' Simon asked.

Harton shook his head. 'No, I gather he's got everything pretty well tied up. We can only be sure, of course, when we see what the next couple of days produce.'

'Your wife, David, is an intelligent woman,' said Charles reflectively. He seemed not to relish the thought.

'Intelligent? Julia? Oh, come, Charles. A certain element of cunning, maybe – but instinctive, not intelligent. And too spite-orientated to be effective in the long term.'

'You are taking a subjective attitude, David. We have to view this thing companywise. And I must stress again that the company has been placed in an awkward position.'

'One could almost say an extremely invidious position,' added Simon.

'Yes, but not by me.'

'By whom, then, David?' The question came gently and with no trace of rhetorical overtone.

'Well, this wretched man Tring, primarily. I mean, we all know that.'

'You were his immediate employer,' Simon said.

'Now look: if we're going to talk about basic responsibility, I think we might start with R.I.P. . . . Who invented *that* bloody concept?'

'David . . .' The reproof was quiet but firm. 'Matters have gone past the stage when there might have been any point in assessing blame. What is all-important now is to build a wall – an impenetrable wall – round the reputation of the company. You mentioned something just now, David. I didn't quite catch it, actually. Simon didn't either. But from now on we all are going to have to be very careful indeed about what we say – in public and in private.'

'I couldn't agree more, Charles.' Harton signalled to the loitering Mr Maddox and ordered brandies.

Simon spoke. 'Reverting to what Rothermere said about Mrs Harton, there are two or three questions I should like to put. The first is this. Has she any knowledge of what Tring was up to before he met with his unfortunate accident?'

'None,' said Harton, bluntly.

'Very well. Two. Is there any way you can think of, any way at all, whereby your wife might grow suspicious about that accident?'

'Put it this way,' said Harton. 'I wouldn't rate her chances as a detective very high. She's got a one-track mind. Once the idea's in her head that I'm going to get 20,000 quid squeezed out of me, she'll be too busy gloating to doubt what she's been told.'

There was silence. Then the man with white hair looked pensively at Harton and said: 'You would appear to have something less than an ideal marriage, David.' His companion looked away and proggled an earhole with his middle finger.

Harton grinned, as if to acknowledge a compliment. 'She's a right bitch.'

'But you do have a replacement in mind?'

'You know I do. That's what this is all about.' Harton saw the admonitory finger, the mouth opening to object; he added at once: 'Apart, I mean, from the main purpose, the company thing. Naturally.'

'Naturally,' echoed Charles, softly.

For a while they sipped their brandy in silence. Harton's offer of cigars was refused by the others. He lit one himself, after cutting the end with elaborate care and going through a rolling and warming ceremony, then laid it aside on an ashtray, where it went out almost immediately.

It was the generally uncommunicative Simon who resumed the discussion. 'Tell me,' he said to Harton, 'your opinion of the local police. You do *have* police here, I suppose?'

'Oh, surely. A full set.'

'Yes, I thought the place would run to something more than a village constable. We've seen the inquest report in your local paper. You actually boast a detective inspector, I gather.'

'Chap called Purbright. Yes.'

'Bumpkin?' This from Charles.

'I wouldn't say that. I've not had much to do with him, actually. He's not in Rotary and he isn't a Mason, but that's not to prove he's a deadhead. My old man loathed him, I remember.'

'Your father?'

'Surgeon. He emigrated to the States last year, having developed a taste for highpriced cock in his old age.'

Simon smiled thinly, without approval. 'Why did your father dislike this inspector?'

'Because the man was inquisitive. He was persistent. I believe he turned up things that my father found professionally embarrassing. The old man was bloody annoyed, and I don't blame him.'

'Let us hope,' said Simon, 'that this village Sherlock of yours hasn't developed a taste for causing embarrassment. We have enough of that to cope with already.'

'No problem,' said Harton. He looked sleek and relaxed, like a four-coloured advertisement for the brandy he cradled in cupped hands and sniffed appreciatively at what he deemed artistic intervals.

'It would be extremely helpful,' said Charles, who had just consulted his watch, 'if one could have absolutely up-to-the-minute knowledge of what the police *have* found out. We don't want to have to wait until the inquest is resumed.'

'Yes, but what *can* they have found out?'

'Oh David, don't be so naive! For one thing, they can find what you and your resourceful girl friend and the cunning Rothermere all failed to find. Look, the train goes in quarter of an hour. If you can't get any back door information out of the Flaxborough police, say so.'

'Very doubtful.'

'Fair enough, David. Let's hope Rothermere delivers, that's all.'

Harton drove them the short distance to the station. The London train was due. He did not wait to see them off.

A chill wind was blowing across the darkening and almost empty Station Square. Harton drove into East Street and headed the car for the Field Street crossing and Queen's Road, where dwelt George and Gladys Lintz, their twenty-five-year-old unmarried daughter, and some fish in an illuminated tank.

Mrs Lintz answered Harton's ring. She was a tubby, tightly permed woman with the habit of constantly checking by fingertip exploration that neck and hair were still within her franchise.

Harton received a smile of welcome. Then, turning her head aside, Mrs Lintz called loudly: 'Bobby-May!' She waited, mouth slightly open, as if to catch an echo. The only sound that reached them was of some televised programme of raised voices, music and applause.

'We were just watching *Guessalong*,' Mrs Lintz explained. It sounded, in her mouth, an occupation as wholesome and universal as breathing. Again she called her daughter, more stridently than before. There came an answering squawk. A door opened and Bobby-May emerged into the lighted hall.

At that distance the girl looked much younger than 25. She was neither noticeably short nor tall, but her movements had an undisciplined, a capricious quality characteristic of a child. Her dress, of a striking emerald green and made of some silkily fluid material, was gathered by a sash and hung at a level just too low to be fashionable. It was the kind of dress that gets called a frock.

'It's Mr Harton, dear.'

'I thought you might like half an hour along at the tennis club, Bobo.' Harton craned forward across the threshold.

'Oh, lovely!' Bobby-May clasped hands and made restless little shuffles. 'Do you mind, Mummy?'

The wide eyes had whites like fresh milk. The irises were richly brown; they scintillated like seal fur.

'Mind? Why should I mind, baby? There's plenty to occupy me. Anyway, Daddy will be back from his Lodge shortly.' Mrs Lintz made to depart, then paused and turned towards Harton. She looked very pleased with life. 'We were just watching *Guessalong*,' she told him in a loud whisper, wrinkling her nose in intimation of the magnitude of the treat he was missing out there in the cold. Then she hurried away.

Bobby-May ran to Harton, pulled him inside by the arm and closed the door. She nuzzled against his chest. He bent and brushed his lips among her shiny, liquorice-black curls.

Suddenly she threw her head back. Harton had to jerk away his face to avoid a blow on the nose. When he looked at her again, her eyes were closed, her lips pursed imperiously. He kissed her, but she broke away almost at once. 'Shan't be a jiffy.'

Harton watched her race upstairs, green sash flying, three-inch heels tottering dangerously. Legs not as good as Julia's. A harder, livelier bottom, though.

In less than a minute, she was back. She carried a pair of racquets and a small sports bag.

'What do you want those for?'

She stared. 'The club, you said.'

'Yes, I *said*. For your dear mum's consumption.'

'Half an hour's prac, David. Go on. Please.' She ran a finger, plump and creamy white, along the line of the pattern of his shirt.

'All right. If the indoor court's free.'

Her eyes flicked shut; the rosebud mouth was offered. He glanced down the hall to the door whence *Guessalong* noises issued, then chanced a man-of-the-world response with lips and tongue-tip. Bobby-May reacted with immediate rigidity and a vacuum lock that reeled his tongue into her mouth like a hose at fire practice.

The embrace lasted nearly two minutes, during which Bobby-May made little growling noises in the back of her throat. When Harton slid his hand over a breast, she grasped it at once and pulled it away, at the same time giving a pro-hibitory head-shake. The effect of this was to aggravate the ache he had begun to feel at the root of his tongue.

She disengaged without warning and ran to throw open the door through which her mother had passed. A racquet whirled in farewell. ''Bye, Mums. Off for an hour's prac.'

In the car, the girl stretched, sighed happily and drew her legs beneath her in a sideways squatting posture.

'You don't really want tennis practice tonight, do you?' he asked.

She was looking across at him speculatively. 'Where's Awful Julia?'

'Awful Julia's out.'

'How do you know Awful Julia's out? I thought you always worked late on Thursday nights.'

He started the engine. 'I've not been home, if that's what you mean. But I do happen to know that Awful Julia is not there, my sweet.'

For a little while, they drove in silence. Over the crossing. Right at the East Street junction and left into Corporation Street. Many of the shop windows were lighted still, but there was no one to look into them except an occasional group of teenagers, sauntering along, tugging at one another, breaking and re-forming, laughing, jeering, leaning against the wind, aimless.

'David . . .'

'Sweetheart?'

'What time will Awful Julia be back?'

'Why do you ask, lover?'

'I was just thinking. We could make do with twenty minutes' prac. Well, I did have a knockabout this afternoon, actually, so.'

'So?'

'So we could go along to your place afterwards for a little while. If Awful Julia's not there, I mean.'

'She won't be.'

Bobby-May gazed dreamily through the windscreen into the middle distance. 'When you've got your divorce, you know,' she said, 'I shall let you possess me utterly.' The last word was delivered with an emphatic stiffening of her throat and chin. Then she relaxed, as if to mark a complete change of subject, and said: 'If you like – and if Awful Julia doesn't turn up – I may let you play our bagpipes-in-the-forest game.'

Harton gave her a fond glance and took his hand from the wheel to squeeze her thigh.

'But remember . . .' She pretended to look stern.

'Yes, sweet?'

'No biteys this time.'

'Scout's honour.'

Chapter Ten

EVERY COMMUNITY SEEMS TO NEED TO DIVIDE ITS history into manageable parcels. Before the Flood and after. Before and after the Conquest. Pre-war and post-war. The policemen of Flaxborough, or those of them at least who had had occasion to deal with death, habitually sliced the past into two sections, uneven in size and of utterly different connotations.

The first, and larger, was The Old Man's Time.

The second was Since Amblesby, or Now That The Old Bugger's Gone.

Sir Albert Amblesby, the senile, scrawny, shambling, agate-eyed lawyer who had confused and terrified inquest witnesses for nearly half a century, had died – still in his office of coroner – in 1974: choked, it was said, upon the honour of knighthood belatedly bestowed for the political skulduggery of his long-gone prime, as a dehydrated miser may choke upon a rich tit-bit.

His successor, another solicitor, James Bell Cannon, was a much younger and less malevolent man.

The coroner's officer, Sergeant Bill Malley, was glad of Cannon's correct attitude towards the grieving and distressed.

But sometimes he missed the challenge of the late Sir Albert's wickedness and the satisfaction he had gained in thwarting it. Cannon was careful, proper, dull. His officer felt like a Saint George turned chauffeur.

So it was that when, on Friday morning, the analyst's final report on the contents of Robert Tring's stomach was delivered by hand at Flaxborough Police Station, Malley acquainted Mr Cannon with the findings before taking the report to Purbright. It was a piece of punctiliousness that would have been unthinkable in The Old Man's Time.

Cannon received the summary gravely. He said that it would appear to complicate the issue somewhat. When was the inquest due to be resumed?

'September twenty-second, sir. Ten days.'

'Very well. We shall just have to see what else turns up, Sergeant. If a further adjournment is necessary, I don't doubt that Mr Purbright will make application at the proper time.'

And he restored his attention to a nice meaty bit of conveyancing.

Malley found the inspector studying another analytical report. This, although issuing from the same laboratory, had been brought round a little later. It looked a good deal briefer than the first.

'Not very helpful,' remarked Purbright, handing the single sheet to Malley. 'It's the whisky.'

'Nothing?'

'Nothing very exciting. The sample was too small – as we thought it would be. I hadn't the heart to disappoint poor old Johnson, though, after he'd carried that bit of bottle corner all the way here from the Market Place.'

Malley passed over his report in silent exchange. Both read for a while. The Sergeant, finishing first, waited.

When Purbright looked up, it was to give Malley a pout of meaningful inquiry. 'So the odds are that Digger was nobbled?'

'That's what it looks like.'

.'Oh, dear.'

Malley shrugged. 'He wasn't a very lovable character, mind. Not Digger.'

'Oh, I'm well aware of that, Bill. It's me I'm sorry for. I'm due to see Mr Chubb in five minutes. He thinks the only thing we have on hand at the moment is the Police Houses Chrysanthemum Competition.'

Which was true. The chief constable, himself a diligent gardener, believed horticulture to be an almost perfectly suitable pursuit for policemen off duty. Its simple symbolism could not be bettered. A rose was an honest life; a cucumber a useful one. Canker and mildew were the crimes to which weak and foolish men would soon fall victim if the police did not go round with spray and secateur. Flaxborough, fortunately, was fairly free of infestation.

'Morning, Mr Purbright.' Mr Chubb turned from his contemplation of the big, oak-cased aneroid barometer on his office wall after giving the glass one final tap with a knuckle.

'The death of Robert Tring,' proclaimed the inspector, hoping that brusqueness would forestall mention of chrysanthemums.

'Tring?' A second's pause. 'Ah, the youth who fell out of some aerial contrivance at the fair.' Mr Chubb indicated a chair for Purbright, then walked to the window, where he continued to stand, curator-like, for the rest of the interview.

'You will remember, sir, that the inquest was opened for evidence of identification. Dr Heineman also appeared, but only to give the actual cause of death.'

'*Only?* How do you mean, Mr Purbright? I should have thought that determining the cause of death was Heineman's entire function.'

'In the ordinary course of events, yes. But there were certain circumstances that he noticed during the post-mortem investigation which struck him as odd. They are included in his full report, but he agreed there would be no point in mentioning them in advance of the analyst's findings. I do have the analyst's report now, sir.'

'I have the impression that something about alcohol came up at the inquest. Heineman didn't keep that back.'

'He had no choice. The Q.C. for the fairground people drew it out in cross-examination. He wanted to suggest irresponsible behaviour on Tring's part, of course.'

Mr Chubb sniffed. 'That shouldn't take much establishing. Very unruly lot round there, I believe.'

'The Tring family are not notably conformist, sir. On the other hand, Robert – or Digger, as they call him – never got into trouble through drinking, let alone drugs.'

'Drugs?' The chief constable looked nervous. He was not by nature an imaginative man, but he once had attended a Home Office film show on the subject that had so harrowed him that he could not now pass herbalist Gingold's shop in East Street without half-expecting a fuddle of junkies to reel from its doorway.

'Heineman noticed some dilation of pupil, sir,' Purbright explained. 'I don't need to tell you, of course, that it is a symptom of narcotic poisoning.'

Mr Chubb's anxiety was clearly increasing. 'Do you mean to tell me, inspector, that Tring was poisoned? I thought it was the fall that killed him.'

'So it was, sir. But he had been drugged first. By . . .' Purbright quickly found the appropriate section of the analysis – 'By two point seven milligrams of hyoscine hydrobromide.'

The Chief Constable looked grave. Hyoscine hydrobromide had a peculiarly menacing sound. 'Where would he get hold of that?' he asked, putting just enough emphasis on the final word to suggest actual knowledge of what it was.

'I have no idea, sir,' Purbright admitted. He added, off-handedly: 'Apart from the two obvious sources, of course.'

Chubb lacked his inspector's advantage of having chatted over the phone half an hour previously with the branch manager of Boots. He waited a moment, then yielded. 'Those sources being?'

'Two types of proprietary medicine, sir, both unrestrictedly on sale, I understand. One is a tablet for the relief of menstrual pain; the other is intended to prevent motion sickness – a so-called travel pill, in fact.'

'In that case, the man could have taken the stuff himself. Even an overdose by accident. They are not too bright in that district, you know.'

Purbright knew better than to dispute the chief constable's method of assessment by address. He said merely: 'It was a fairly substantial overdose – probably ten tablets or more.'

'Of the travel sickness stuff, you mean?'

'I doubt if even a man living in Abdication Avenue would suppose himself to be suffering from period pains, sir.'

'Perhaps not,' conceded Mr Chubb, impassively. He frowned at his finger ends. 'What does this hyoscine whatsitsname do? In that sort of quantity.'

'I'm told the effects would vary a good deal from person to person. There would almost certainly be excitement, though, to begin with, quickly followed by loss of control and even collapse.'

The chief constable sighed. 'I suppose this is all part of what they call getting kicks nowadays. It seems a pity, though, that a grown man has to play the fool on a roundabout. Fairs are for children. This sort of thing spoils them.'

'We do not know,' Purbright pointed out, 'that Tring took the drug of his own volition. There was another man with him on the ride. Girls in the car behind say that both men were having drinks from the same bottle, but Tring more than his companion.'

'Who was this other fellow?'

'He hasn't come forward, sir. And no one so far has been able to identify him. The fairground attendant who took their money remembers the pair, but only because of the things they were wearing – their motor-cycling outfits. He didn't get a look at the face of either.'

By this time, Mr Chubb was wearing that expression of mournful omniscience which betokened an inability to make sense of what he had been told. Purbright recognised that he need offer only a couple more pieces of confusing evidence for the chief constable suddenly to consult his watch, express alarm lest he be late for an undefined appointment, and hasten away to the sanctuary of the greenhouse at his home in Queen's Road.

'A bottle,' persisted the inspector, 'which might well be the one from which Tring and his friend were taking nips, fell among the crowd just before Tring's body came down. It was smashed, of course, but P.C. Johnson very sensibly collected the pieces, including a corner of the base that still held a few drops of whisky. I asked the analyst to do what he could with it.'

Purbright glanced at the second report before replacing it in his pocket. 'The sample wasn't big enough to yield much information, but there's no doubt it was whisky, or something very similar. One queer thing, sir. An unusually high proportion of sugar.'

'What about that drug, though?' Mr Chubb inquired. 'The hyoscine?' He began to move a hand towards the watch pocket of his waistcoat.

The inspector shook his head. 'Too small a sample, sir. It's the sugar reading that could be significant, though.'

'Oh, yes, Mr Purbright?' Finger and thumb closed upon the silver watch chain.

'The motion sickness pills I mentioned earlier consist mainly of a chewable, palatable base – some kind of sugary substance. Ten or a dozen dissolved in part of a quartern bottle of whisky would account for what the analyst found. Of course, I don't need to tell you that a straight malt is not normally sweetened for drinking.'

The chief constable perceptibly paled. It was two or three seconds before he hauled up his slim silver watch and muttered 'Gracious me, road safety committee.'

'You will wish me to push ahead with inquiries as a matter of some urgency, sir?' Purbright rose to his feet.

'Certainly, Mr Purbright. If there is anything further you wish to ask me, please don't hesitate.'

'Thank you, sir.' Almost at the door, Purbright turned. 'One small point, sir. Glenmurren whisky is a fairly unusual brand, I understand; do you happen to know anyone who buys it? We shall be asking the various suppliers, but short cuts are always appreciated.'

Mr Chubb stared ruminatively at the opposite wall. He shook his head. 'It does ring a bell.' A pause. 'But rather distantly.'

Purbright grasped the door handle, then saw the chief constable raise his hand.

'Gwill,' said Mr Chubb, very affirmatively and with satisfaction. 'Gwill. Old Marcus. He used to drink the stuff. I remember they kept some in for him at the club before he passed on.'

Purbright's ease of recall of the 'passing on' in question was not surprising. The bizarre electrocution in 1958 of Marcus Gwill, proprietor of the *Flaxborough Citizen*, had provided the inspector with his first murder case.

'Mind you,' added Mr Chubb, 'I can't see that poor old Marcus's preferences can have any bearing on this business of yours. Just one of those odd little memories.'

'Yes, sir. Funny old world.' And Purbright departed before Mr Chubb could decide whether the remark had been philosophic or fatuous.

Back in his own office, he found Detective Sergeant Love in wait, looking pleased.

'We've been trying to get hold of you,' Love announced. 'A missing person case has turned up.'

'Do you mean that a disappearance has become apparent?'

'No, it's this tottie. She's gone.'

Purbright closed his eyes and lowered himself gently into the chair behind his desk. 'Look, Sid – one thing at a time. First of all, I want a whole lot more questions asked about the Tring business. I'll help you make a list, then we can get the infantry organised.'

A programme of inquiry was devised. The main task would be the thankless one of questioning Tring's known associates in an effort to find the identity of his companion on what Love, a reckless coiner of journalistic phrases, was pleased to term his 'death ride'. Also there would need to be a closer and more persistent examination of the man's activities both at his place of work and elsewhere, on the principle, as expressed by the sergeant, that 'nobody gets done in without asking for it'. And lastly – again the definition of objective was owed to Love's earthy percipience – there was that 'pricey Scotch jollop' to be traced to source.

'And now,' Purbright said after disposition of manpower had been sketched out, 'what is this about a missing tottie?'

Chapter Eleven

UPON MR AND MRS M. H. ROTHERMERE, OF HAMPSTEAD, London, emerging from connubial slumber on the first floor of the Jesmondia Hotel, attended the proprietoress in person, with breakfast tray borne in her wake by her husband, the major.

Mrs Cartwright gave a featherlight knock with one hand while with the other she peremptorily pass-keyed entry.

Mr Rothermere, hair and beard tousled, hauled himself by the bedclothes to a sitting position. He looked a good deal alarmed for some seconds, then noticed that Julia was making semi-conscious stirrings beside him. He solicitously replaced over her naked breast the sheet his own rising had disturbed.

Mrs Cartwright opened the curtains and inspected the scene with quicksilver eye before beckoning the major through the doorway. He set the tray down on the floor in the corner furthest from the bed.

Mr Rothermere said thank you. Julia pretended to be still asleep. The major, who wore a loose drill jacket over the shirt and trousers of the night before, stood by the door for a few moments staring at Julia and the tray by turns, as if hopeful that she might suddenly dash to retrieve it. His wife bustled him out.

In the corridor, she looked at him thoughtfully and said: 'It's him. You're quite right. It's Mr Hive.'

'Said it was.'

'Yes, but he didn't have the beard before. Just the moustache. A beard suits him.'

'Thought he'd retired.'

'Detectives never retire.'

The major lifted the corner of his lip derisively. 'Detective? The man's a professional co-respondent. Always was. A blasted paid bed-jumper.'

'Used to be.' Mrs Cartwright was shaking her head. '*Used* to be. And even then he was very select. *Very* select. He once told me that this hotel was very handy for the Sandringham trade. I expect that's why he's here now. And why he's not let on to me who he is. Because of *her*.'

Speculation and dispute continued to the end of the corridor and down the stairs. Then other breakfasts demanded attention, other awakenings.

Mr Rothermere, formerly Hive, told Julia, on her return to bed with the tray, that he sincerely valued womanly independence and never tried to erode it by displays of pseudo-chivalry. He also told her – to her even greater gratification – that she picked her way amongst furniture with the grace of

97

the nude eighteen-year-old Indonesian waitress he once had seen at the home of Godfrey Winn.

They balanced the tray between them and surveyed its contents. There were sausages, four fried eggs, some rashers of bacon, mushrooms, fried bread, a rack of toast, butter in a dish, marmalade and honey, and a large pot of coffee.

'Among the many excellent attributes of the English,' remarked Mr Rothermere, spearing sausages, 'is their recognition of adultery as healthy exercise.'

'We are supposed to be married,' Julia observed.

'Mm-yes.' He slid a couple of eggs on to her plate and added bacon. 'Hampstead address, though. Sinful connotations. How nice to have really crisp fried bread.'

'Oh, it is, it is. I hate it when they fry only one side and leave the blank side down on the plate to get steamy and soggy.'

'God, yes. They used to do that at Marlborough. I've never forgotten. Nor forgiven.'

'Hotel, was it?'

Mr Rothermere saw innocence in the eyes above the raised forkful of bacon and mushroom and quelled his conditioned reflexes. Instead of murmuring '*School, actually,*' he nodded.

Julia, happily determined to prolong the novelty of conversation at breakfast, indicated the butter with her knife. 'How much more appetising,' she said, 'than those dreadful little foil-wrapped tablets.'

'Indeed, yes.' He sought with his eyes the bowl of demerara. 'And no wrapped individual sugar cubes, you notice. They always look to me like instruments of polite euthanasia.'

Julia thought: How nice and warm he is, under the bedclothes; and not forever shuffling about.

Mr Rothermere thought: There is a graciousness about this woman that I like: when my stomach rumbled just now, she pretended to look pleased, as if by birdsong.

And as they ate and drank and discoursed, her left foot and

his right came together and little toe linked companionably in little toe.

They rose and dressed at half-past nine. In the hotel lounge they were scrutinised by two women and an elderly clergyman, all looking worried; and by a family in chairs at the window: father, mother and two adolescent boys, whose general expression was of gloomy pique, as if they had been put into quarantine.

'Anyone for beach cricket?' Mr Rothermere jocosely inquired of the room at large.

The clergyman and his escort quickly looked away from him and froze in contemplation of one another's knitwear.

The two boys, reddening horribly at the sudden eruption of a loony into their lives, gazed down at their hands and had breathing trouble, on noticing which their father went red also. He leaned forward, pulled ears, and hissed admonition, leaving his wife to offer sole response to Mr Rothermere's invitation. This she did by smiling flickeringly (loose connection? wondered Mr Rothermere, compassionately) and saying that it was nice of him, Mr – er – but not just now, thanks all the same, Mr – er . . .

'Rothermere,' he supplied, beaming. 'I own the *Daily Mail*.'

The respiration of the smaller of the two boys grew suddenly more erratic. He began to wet himself.

Julia tugged at her companion's arm. 'You have some business to attend to, remember? And it's a long way to Flaxborough.'

They went out into the lobby.

'What are you going to do?' he asked her.

'Some shopping. And I should like to walk along the beach if it's not too cold.'

'Don't forget that you have been done away with. At least remember not to ask a policeman anything.'

She grinned, but almost at once looked serious again. 'It won't come to that.' She took hold of his sleeve. 'Look,

99

Mortimer – you're not to carry this thing too far. Scare the bugger a little, certainly; I don't mind that. But I couldn't go through with the real thing. You did realise that, didn't you?'

He took her hand. 'Of course. He must feel that we are ruthless, though. That is why you must stay out of the way. Leave it to me to keep up the pressure.' And Mr Rothermere made wheel-turning motions with his free hand and looked as grim as Captain Ahab having his leg off.

'No police, then?'

'No police. I promise.' Ahab was gone and back was Edward the Seventh, kindly, genial, reliable.

Julia posted a quick, schoolgirlish kiss in the gap between beard and moustache and walked lightly to the door. She looked back. 'You'll ring tonight?'

'Without fail, dear lady.'

She smiled and was gone.

Mr Rothermere went over to the reception counter, where Mrs Cartwright had been straining, under cover of busy-ness with ledgers, to catch what she could of the conversation. He bowed, holding his silver-grey, curly brimmed hat close to his diaphragm, and handed her the room key.

'I shall be away for a day or two – probably until after the weekend – but I'm sure my wife will be consoled by the excellence of your cuisine.'

Mrs Cartwright bobbed and shuffled with pleasure. She looked more than ever like a parrot on a perch.

'As soon as we saw her,' said Mrs Cartwright, her head a little on one side as if inviting a scratch, 'my husband and I thought what a nice lady. Mrs Rothermere, I mean.'

Mr Rothermere gave another small bow.

'Do you know who she puts me in mind of?' Mrs Cartwright leaned forward a little.

'I have no idea.'

The beak came nearer. Softly: 'Princess Anne.'

There was a long pause. Then Mr Rothermere clapped upon

his head the curly brimmed hat and with one tug set it at a jaunty rake.

'I am confident,' he said, 'that among all the excellent attributes of this establishment, discretion is not the least noteworthy.'

My God, thought Mrs Cartwright, I've put my finger on something there. Her thoughts raced ahead. The Sandringham Room – no, the Royal Suite – well, why not? – thirty per cent surcharge . . .

Mr Rothermere drove south at a gentle pace, enjoying the softly undulating Norfolk countryside, mistily gilded by weak September sunshine. But when he reached Norwich, instead of taking the western road that would have led him to Wisbech and thence across the fenlands on the way to Flaxborough, he chose the south-bound A11 and was soon being sluiced along in the traffic for London.

Just north of Woodford, he turned off the main road and penetrated a maze of suburban avenues. The Fiat finally drew up at the gate of a three-bedroomed semi-detached villa with a loggy name board above its door proclaiming the dwelling to be 'MAYSTEAD' (cleverly commemorative of its inmates, Maisie and Ted Robinson, art dealers).

Mrs Robinson only was at home, her husband having gone to Walthamstow to replenish their stocks of plain paper wrappers. She greeted Mr Rothermere with the utmost affability and said goodness me, wasn't it a long time but, my, he was looking a hundred per cent.

Mr Rothermere made suitable response, helped himself eagerly to Mrs Robinson's offering of home-made scones and raspberry jam, and announced that he had brought a little commission – a somewhat delicate montage job upon which much depended.

Declaring that she liked nothing better than a challenge, Mrs Robinson accepted the camera her visitor had brought, together with an envelope containing a photograph of the late

Robert Digby Tring, motor-cyclist, and retired to the rustic garden shed that housed, unsuspected by neighbours, a splendidly equipped darkroom and photographic laboratory.

Mr Rothermere took a turn in the garden. Ted's dahlias were at their best and were rivalled only by a double row of huge shaggy chrysanthemums, white, yellow and bronze, each lashed to a neat but sturdy stake, a sort of floral Andromeda. He admired the Nymphs' Grotto and the Merry Fisher Lad and the big model windmill, painted bright blue and red, with sails that really went round whenever the wind blew from Wanstead, and he recognised Maisie's handiwork in the Lord's Prayer done in musselshell mosaic round the concrete base of the bird table.

'Hey, these are pretty dinky, Mortimer.'

The door of the darkroom had opened, presumably after whatever period of segregation had been necessary for the development of Mr Rothermere's film roll.

He peered in. Mrs Robinson was rocking something in a flat white dish. 'Anything come out?' he asked carelessly.

'Nice as ninepence, all of them but one. Who's your modelling lady?'

'Just someone I happened to meet at this ridiculous grouse shoot.'

He explained his requirements. Mrs Robinson, who wore a housewifely apron, tested solution temperatures with the tip of her little finger and timed immersions by counting 'dickory one, dickory two, dickory three . . .' seemed to find nothing difficult or exceptionable in the task. Mr Rothermere left her humming happily over her tanks and enlargers and went back into the house, where he poured himself a glass of port and relaxed on the big green sofa in the bay window.

In less than half an hour, Mrs Robinson entered the room and handed him three small prints. Mr Rothermere gave them long and admiring examination. He looked up.

'You know something? – these are quite incredibly good – I mean, incredibly.'

'You old soft soaper,' said Mrs Robinson, pushing him in playful reproof. 'You're as bad as Lucy Teatime when it comes to laying it on.'

'Which reminds me,' said Mr Rothermere, raising one finger, 'I must give Lucy a call before I leave her neighbourhood.' He put the prints into their envelope and slipped it in his pocket.

'Give her our love,' said Maisie.

Mr Rothermere stood before the mirror and preened his beard and moustache with the curled forefinger of his right hand.

Mrs Robinson regarded him thoughtfully. 'You've not married again, then, Mortimer?'

'Not recently.'

'Are you sure you cannot stay to lunch? Ted will be very sorry to have missed you.'

Protesting equal regret, he took his leave. At the gate he turned, waved to the little pinafored figure in the doorway of 'Maystead', and blew her a kiss as gallantly as a recalled hussar. He left the gate open for the postman who had just arrived at that moment with the Robinsons' not inconsiderable pile of mid-day mail.

Mr Rothermere drove back towards the main road until he saw a public telephone box. He pulled up beside it, made a brief call, and resumed his journey. At Ware he bought petrol and made for Stevenage and the A1. He reached Newark a little after four o'clock and by half-past five he was exploring the interior of a pie in the parlour of the Waggon and Horses public house in Pennick village. Discovering nothing overtly dangerous in the pie, he anaesthetised it with mustard and quickly devoured it. He was still hungry, so he ordered another pie. He had almost consumed this one when someone entered the bar and sat on the trestle opposite. It was David Harton.

Mr Rothermere leaned towards him, indicated the remains of the pie with his fork, and said very earnestly: 'Look, you must try one of these; they are quite remarkably good. Why don't you let me order you one?'

By his framing of the question, by his manner, by the confidential pitch of his voice – somehow Mr Rothermere contrived to convey the impression that not only was he the sole agent for the dispensing of pies in Pennick but in all probability the patentee of the process of their manufacture.

Harton declined. 'Let me get you a drink,' he offered in compensation.

Mr Rothermere considered solemnly, then nodded. 'Half a pint of ordinary bitter beer. Thank you.' He popped the last bit of pie-crust into his mouth and dabbed his lips with a handkerchief.

When Harton returned with drinks, Mr Rothermere unobtrusively handed him one of the three prints fabricated by Mrs Robinson.

'That should solve your little problem.'

Harton stared stonily at the photograph for some seconds, his mouth tight. A muscle at the side of his jaw twitched. High in the cheek a patch of skin flushed darkly.

'This man,' expounded Mr Rothermere, 'is probably the finest photographic technician in London. He did the Kennedy assassination picture that beat the news agencies by eight minutes – and without leaving his studio.'

Harton frowned, questioning.

Airily, very rapidly – as if anxious not to insult his hearer's intelligence by too clearly articulating the obvious – Mr Rothermere murmured: 'Computerised filing system, three buttons – who – where – what – then advanced montage technique . . . not difficult, not to this man.'

Harton looked at him. 'Did *you* get her to pose like this?'

'Now look, you must be absolutely objective . . .'

'Did you?'

'I think she was a little intoxicated at the time. It was all quite impersonal, anyway.'

Harton's grin – the boyish one – was suddenly there. 'My dear chap, I'm not criticising. This is just right. Great.'

'Our mutual employer,' said Mr Rothermere after a pause, 'is concerned, I understand, that you should get your divorce as quickly and cleanly as possible. That is how that Charles fellow put it, anyhow; he didn't seem to see any contradiction between cleanliness and fake adultery.'

'It's a very sensitive field, dog food,' said Harton. 'I mean, hell, I couldn't care less, but here's a market that can go up or down by a million at the wag of a tail on television. Customers of that kind are terribly fussy about morals.'

'Your wife would readily settle for reasonable alimony. Wouldn't that be less complicated? Less risky?'

'Christ! I know her "reasonable". She's cunning enough to have worked out her own estimate of what value Cultox puts on the fair name of its executives. She'd bleed us white.'

Mr Rothermere drummed his fingers on the side of his tankard and ruminatively inspected its depths. 'I rather fancy,' he said, 'that I could name a likely figure.'

'Don't tell me the bitch got you to come here and bargain for her.'

'Not at all. She believes precisely what I was engaged to persuade her to believe.'

At once, Harton gestured with open hand. 'That her poor sod of a husband was going to be framed for knocking her off. She'd believe that, all right. And love it.'

'As a general rule,' said Mr Rothermere, 'I counsel against complicated plots. In this case, it seemed that something elaborate – a little bizarre, even – was more likely to appeal to your wife's particular mentality. I have been proved right. But now that she has responded as planned, my advice is that she be offered prompt accommodation.'

'I don't follow you, friend.' The slightly pained brow above the open smile bespoke a desire to understand.

'In short,' said Mr Rothermere, 'I suggest you settle at once. You have the lever you wanted – the photograph, which Mrs Harton has not seen, incidentally, but which I am sure she would not care to have to contest in court – so you can afford to be generous.'

'Generous to what extent?'

'Listen, I think she would accept fifteen thousand. Offer twelve and I'll work from there. I do have some little experience in the mediation business, as you know.' Mr Rothermere gave a small self-deprecatory shrug. 'At least I shouldn't have gelignite or Arabic idiom to contend with on this occasion.'

Harton took a couple of seconds to allow the image conjured by the latest of Mr Rothermere's potent non-sequiturs to clear. Then he scowled and leaned forward. Slowly and emphatically, he said:

'That woman was prepared to see me dragged into court on a murder charge and quite possibly be put away for life. The only accommodation, as you put it, that I'm prepared to offer her is what she wanted me to have – a prison cell.'

Almost before Harton had finished speaking, Mr Rothermere was pouting disagreement and shaking his head. 'No, no, no, no. You have misread the situation. I'm sorry, but you really have. She would never have persevered with that absurd pretence. It was a game, nothing more, and she knew that.'

'She is a murderous bitch.'

'Oh, come now . . .'

'She is a murderous bitch. And we are going to see that she is recognised and treated as one. Right?' The brittle politeness of Harton's smile proclaimed, for the first time in the interview, the relationship between employer and hired man.

Chapter Twelve

'I DON'T CARE WHAT SHE'S DONE, INSPECTOR. I JUST want her home again. If she's in trouble – well, we'll have to see what can be done to help her. Nothing's so desperately bad that human beings can't get together to try and put it right.'

'How true, sir,' said Purbright, never one to dispute a worthy sentiment. But he added, before Harton had time to express another, that he would be interested to hear what he supposed the 'trouble' encountered by Mrs Harton was likely to be.

The interview was taking place in the drawing-room of the Hartons' house in Oakland. It was Saturday morning, a time which normally would have been at Purbright's disposal for shopping with his wife or mending a fence or changing library books or indeed any of the ordinary weekend activities that bring even policemen in Flaxborough back into circulation as citizens and neighbours. But that could not be helped. Julia Harton was the daughter of a headmaster and a J.P. and the wife of a substantial employer. Her vanishing was a matter that demanded the immediate attention and attendance of a senior officer.

'Trouble?' Harton repeated the word as if putting it up for examination. He considered, then shrugged. 'Yes I think we must assume that she is in trouble. She would not otherwise go off without explanation of any kind.'

'But doesn't it seem unlikely that she *has* gone? In the sense of taking a journey, I mean. Her car is still at the factory.'

'That is true. But there are other means of going away. Public transport, such as it is. A lift with a friend.'

'You make it sound as if you believe your wife left deliberately, sir.'

'Well, I do. Yes.' Harton looked surprised. 'What else should I believe, inspector?'

'Do you rule out forcible abduction?'

'Kidnapping? Oh, no; surely not. Not in Flaxborough.' Harton shook his head. 'To be quite honest, I could wish that were the explanation. Then it would simply be a matter of money.'

'Demands are sometimes very extravagant – especially when someone such as an industrialist is involved.'

'The money would be raised,' said Harton, quietly and simply. 'Julia was not kidnapped, though,' he added in exactly the same tone.

Purbright waited a few moments.

'When you telephoned yesterday to report that your wife had not been seen since Thursday evening,' he said, 'my sergeant advised you – and I should have done the same – to make inquiries among her friends and members of her family before assuming that something had happened to her. By now, you have done that, of course.'

'Of course. Absolutely no result. Nothing.'

'Do you know if she took anything with her – clothing, luggage of any kind? Have you been able to check that?'

'A suitcase, I think, but I'm not certain. I mean, one doesn't keep an inventory of these things.'

'No, sir. And clothing? Perhaps that would be even more difficult to be sure about, though?'

Harton smiled in a withdrawn, regretful way. 'I am not the most observant of husbands, I'm afraid, inspector. There are many things about Julia I notice rather late in the day, if at all. Not very flattering.' Suddenly, Harton struck his knee with his clenched fist. 'God! I can't understand how women put up with our damned insensitivity.'

'Does that mean, Mr Harton, that you believe your wife has ceased to put up with what you consider your failings? That she has left you, in fact?'

'Sounds very simple, doesn't it,' said Harton, mournfully.

'If it were that simple, you would have gone to your solicitor and not the police. Don't you think, sir, that it's time you told me what you really think has happened? What you *fear* has happened, rather?'

Harton looked up. 'You're very perceptive, inspector. Fear – yes, I suppose it's there. But I couldn't sketch it out for you.

It's quite formless. You know? What I can do, though, is to tell you certain things – very odd things, I think they are – that have puzzled and worried me a great deal, especially since Julia disappeared.' He rose from his chair and went to the sideboard. 'Are you sure you won't have anything to drink?'

Purbright saw him uncork a bottle of sweet sherry. There were several other bottles and a decanter. 'Not in that sense; no, sir. I should appreciate a cup of tea, though, if it's not too much trouble.'

'Surely.' Harton moved to the door. 'I'll ask my woman to get you one.'

Mrs Cutlock came into the room five minutes later. She ogled Purbright with enormous curiosity while pretending to look for a suitable landing for the tray she held. The interview was suspended until she could no longer affect blindness to the empty and adequate table between the two men. As she was leaving, Harton called to her:

'Oh, Mrs Cutlock, you'll remember what I said about the kitchen, won't you? Not to move anything – just to leave it exactly as it was when you came.'

'Don't worry. I heard what you said.' Mrs Cutlock looked offended. She resolved to tell that yellow-thatched pollis about the Hartons' slanging match as soon as she could get him on his own.

Harton told Purbright that the significance of what he had said to his woman would be clear a little later. In the meantime he had some rather, well, some rather distasteful things to tell him. They concerned his marriage.

'Mark you, though,' he said, 'I want to be absolutely fair. I do not consider myself a wronged husband or anything of that kind. Whatever has happened is attributable to shortcomings of my own. What those shortcomings are, I have never been sensitive enough – perhaps I ought to say intelligent enough – to understand.'

Purbright put milk and sugar in his cup and tipped the pot

experimentally. The tea was of a reasonably amber shade but several leaves bobbed at once to the surface and remained swirling there, mutely accusing Mrs Cutlock of having neglected, in her haste to return and overhear more of the conversation, to boil the water properly.

'This matter of understanding,' said Harton, frowning at his sherry. 'You can guess the area in which mine was most likely to fall short. I was an only child and I had the sort of monastic upbringing that is still the norm at public school. Not to put too fine a point on it, I had been led to regard sex as a function, not an art.'

Harton silently watched the inspector chase errant tea leaves with his spoon and land them, like dead fish, on the saucer's edge. 'You must think me very naive,' he said.

'Not particularly, sir. I appreciate that you are preparing to tell me something that has shocked you. It is perfectly sensible of you to make me understand how susceptible to shock you happen to be.'

Harton smiled gratefully and took several short, quick sips of his drink.

'My wife and I,' he resumed, 'seemed to get along fairly well until a couple of months ago. I mean, it wasn't one of these starlight and music marriages, admittedly, but we weren't tearing into each other every five minutes, and we had a sort of mutual respect thing. Anyway, I thought she was pretty content, within limits. Mind you, the bed side of it – you know what I mean? – that was definitely short on viability. My fault. Sure. I mean I just had a different sort, a different *degree*, of appetite. She as good as asked me once if we couldn't go out and – you know – do it – in the garden. She said she'd always wanted to, in a deckchair. That shook me. Unreasonable? Prudish? Right. Right. I know. But it's just me. I can't stand freakishness, as we old reactionaries call it. It's like imperfection. To me, a woman has to be unblemished. Listen, you'll think this silly, and I suppose it is, but do you know I couldn't bear to sleep with a person who had a physical defect. Julia's front teeth were a bit crooked when I married her. Once I noticed, I knew she'd have to do something about them or our marriage would crash. She was very understanding, actually; I got my London man to cap them. It cost me a couple of hundred, but there you are. It was that important to me.'

There was a knock at the door, and the head of Mrs Cutlock was introduced.

'All done now, Mr Harton. At least, I think so. Has Mrs Harton anything she wants seeing to? She doesn't seem to be about this morning.'

'My wife is away visiting, Mrs Cutlock. I don't think there will be much point in your coming on Monday. Make it Wednesday, will you?'

'Wednesday. Just as you like. All right – Wednesday.' The head gave Harton a formal nod. Purbright, in contrast, was favoured with one of Mrs Cutlock's most confidential grins. 'Mornin', superintendent,' she said in a husky baritone of admiration. 'Nice to see you on the trail again.'

'What did she mean by that?' asked Harton as soon as the door was shut once more.

'I've no idea, sir. I think perhaps she comes of a family of a naturally cheerful disposition.' Purbright saw no reason to add that the Cutlocks had achieved by long persistence in criminal endeavour that degree of intimacy with the police which looks to the uninformed observer very like comradeship.

'Anyway, now that she's gone I can show you something that has been worrying me a great deal.' Harton drank off the rest of his sherry and walked to the door. His movements, Purbright noticed, were quick and unequivocal; they were those of a man who expected others to follow promptly and to do as they were told. Curious, that hidden area of sexual ingenuousness.

The kitchen looked very clean, almost clinical. As soon as Harton entered it, his manner became a fraction less sure.

Purbright guessed that he was not a man accustomed to, or indeed capable of, looking after himself.

Harton stared around for a moment, then bent and tugged open first one cupboard door, then another. On seeing what lay inside the second – it was immediately beneath the sink – he said, ah, yes, this was it, and pulled out a bundle roughly wrapped in newspaper.

'I was searching round for a saucepan to warm some milk before I went to bed last night, and just happened to look in here. There was this parcel, pushed up towards the back. I wouldn't have taken any notice in the ordinary way, but I spotted this boot heel sticking up through the paper like it is now, and thought, odd place to put boots – whose are they, anyway? So I heaved the stuff out.'

Harton stepped back, and with his hand invited Purbright to examine the parcel.

The inspector squatted beside it and folded back the newspaper layers.

Delicately, he sniffed. A feminine, cosmetic smell was noticeable first, but closer trial brought into prominence a tang of engine fume and oil.

'Not yours, I presume, sir.' He spoke over his shoulder.

'Hardly.'

Purbright transferred in turn to an empty table the tunic, breeches and long boots.

'And you've never seen them before?'

'Not until last night, no.'

Purbright made a careful but not prolonged examination. When he spoke again, he looked directly at Harton.

'You had better tell me what significance you think ought to be attached to these things, Mr Harton. I may be a little obtuse, but I can't pretend to have grasped instantly their relevance to what you have been telling me up to now.'

'Of course not. I wasn't trying to be dramatic or anything of that sort. I'm still pretty confused myself, as a matter of fact. Look, if we can sit down, I'll try and tell you what's been going on.'

'Shall we go back to the other room, then, sir? I'd appreciate another cup of tea.'

'That's all right. I'll fetch the tray.' Harton pointed to a chair and hurried out. The sudden courtesy seemed to Purbright uncharacteristic; it was a measure, perhaps, of the distress the renewed sight of that leather costume had aroused.

When Harton came in again, both men sat at the table. Harton had brought on the tray a second glass of sherry for himself. Purbright poured more tea.

'A few weeks ago,' Harton began, 'my wife picked up acquaintance with a chap at the factory. She used to come through the works sometimes on the way to my office. The men knew who she was, of course, and generally spoke to her.

'This particular fellow, though, fancied himself as a bit of a lady-killer. He was the kind who would say things right out of line just to see what effect they would have. A cheeky bastard, in fact.

'I saw them together one evening just before the end of shift. Not for more than a few seconds, but I noticed how he looked at her – you know, brassy – what I call working-class obstreperous – and I also saw him put his hand on her back, here, low down. And damn me if she didn't look pleased, as if he'd paid her some kind of compliment. I just felt disgusted. I never said anything to her.

'Of course' – Harton looked down at his finger ends and smiled weakly – 'I realise now that I should have felt disgusted at myself, not at poor Julia. I suppose I must have let her get into such a frustrated state that her self-respect wasn't operative any more.'

He looked up again at Purbright, impassively tea-sipping. 'Be that as it may, from about that time our life together was utterly transformed – and in a very nasty way, believe me, inspector. Hostility, sneering, nagging, tears, tempers – and frigidity – my God, such frigidity! *That* I didn't need ask her to explain. I knew.'

Purbright hoped he was not looking as unsympathetic as he felt. A large piece of precious Saturday morning was already lost. Marriage counsellors did not work weekends; why should he?

He set down his cup. 'Look, sir, I don't want to appear indifferent to your domestic difficulties, but my concern – and no one regrets this more than I do – is crime. Before you tell me anything else, I must put the question which perhaps I should have asked at the outset. Have you good reason to suppose that your wife is dead or has come to serious harm, and has not simply left you?'

A look of innocent surprise came over Harton's face.

'My dear inspector, I may be unhappy and confused, but I am still enough of a business man to know better than to waste the time of a professional. No, I don't think Julia is dead – pray God she wouldn't be that desperate – but I do believe she is in very serious trouble.'

'Life and death,' said Purbright drily, 'was a phrase you used, I understand, when you asked the chief constable to send someone to see you.'

'Yes, I did. I think with good reason.' Harton rose and pointed to the clothing. 'These you have seen. Now I have something else to show you.'

He led the way into the hall and began ascending the stairs. Purbright, close behind, noted they they were covered with heavy cream carpet, meticulously cut to fit every contour.

Harton opened a door and went inside. Purbright stood beside him and glanced at the twin beds, as far apart as they would go; at the dressing table and chest of drawers and the cupboards built into the wall; at the great mirror in which was another bedroom, incongruously inhabited by a smartly dressed businessman and a tall police inspector with not very tidy yellow hair and the middle button missing from his ageing broadcloth jacket.

114

Harton moved closer to the dressing table.

'Last night I didn't know what the hell to do. That stuff downstairs – I couldn't make any sense of it, and that worried me. So I began going through all her things. I thought I might find something, some clue to what she was up to. Oh, yes, I knew bloody well she'd been having it off – isn't that what they call it nowadays, having it off? – with that oaf at the plant, but hell, he'd been dead a week so whatever her reason for leaving, it couldn't have been to shack up with him.'

'Just a moment, sir.' Purbright had held up his hand. 'You haven't mentioned so far what this man's name was.'

Harton smiled faintly. 'It ought to be familiar enough to you, inspector, if what our personnel manager tells me about his family is correct. Tring. On the Council estate.'

'Robert Tring?'

'I don't know his first name.'

Purbright shook his head as if dismissing an irrelevancy. 'You were saying, sir?'

Harton moved round in front of him and squatted a little to one side of the dressing table. He pointed. 'This I left until last. It was always something private to her; I didn't have a key.'

Purbright leaned close. Harton was showing him a small drawer, the lowest of three on the left hand side of the dressing table. Some of the rosewood veneer was split away near the keyhole. 'I had to force it,' Harton said. He pulled the drawer out and laid it on the cover of the nearer bed.

Without saying anything, Harton picked up the topmost object in the drawer and handed it to Purbright.

It was an envelope. A slightly grubby, unaddressed, unsealed manilla envelope.

Purbright lifted the flap and took out the photograph it contained. He glanced immediately at Harton and saw that his face was tense and almost white. He motioned him to sit on the edge of the bed.

'It's not very nice,' said Harton, 'to have to show you a thing like that.'

'No, sir.' The simple, gentle negative was kinder than any formally framed expression of regret. Privately, though, Purbright was wondering why Harton had thought it necessary to share knowledge of the photograph.

Then he saw that bluish indentations on the surface of the picture were in fact words. They had been scrawled with a ball-point pen. He tilted the photograph slightly towards the light from the window and read what the words were.

Worth £2000, ducky? Ask your old man.

Purbright indicated them to Harton. 'Crude. But explicit.'

'Certainly.'

'Do you think she made any attempt to raise this sort of money, Mr Harton? Recently, I mean?'

'Not from me.'

'Do you suppose "old man" could mean Mrs Harton's father?'

'I doubt it. He's only a school teacher.'

'Still, it's the implication that matters – the threat of exposure. That's clear enough.'

Harton put forward his little finger, hesitantly, as if wishing to indicate something hateful. 'The boots, you see? The same.'

'Yes, sir; that is my impression, too.'

Angrily, Harton turned away his head. 'By Christ! I wonder if she'd have looked so pleased with herself if she'd known she was posing with a bloody blackmailer!'

Purbright replaced the photograph in the envelope. 'I'll take this with me, if you don't mind, sir. You needn't worry. It will be treated with the very greatest discretion.'

Harton made as if to object, then paused, shrugged. 'Of course, inspector.'

The little drawer was between them on the bed. Purbright bent and looked into it, gently shifting its contents about with one finger.

'What are these, sir?'

Purbright held forward in his palm two pale blue plastic tubes, each about four inches long and fitted with a white cap.

'No idea. It's all her stuff in there. Odds and ends. There was only the photograph that was important, though.'

While Purbright examined the tubes and read what was printed upon them, he addressed Harton in a quiet, almost absent-minded manner.

'Do you have any suggestion to offer, sir, as to why your wife is missing? By "serious trouble" I'm sure you mean something more drastic than running away from the consequences of a rash affair, even if they do include attempted extortion.'

Harton made no reply. Purbright looked up. 'Am I right?'

Harton got up abruptly and strode to the window. He stared out.

'Inspector, I want you to believe that I am only talking to you now because there seems no other way of helping my wife. I would have kept silent – I would have lied – I would have done anything, however stupid, if she had asked me. But she simply ran away, so I have to make my own decision. All I can do is to pass to you such facts as I have, also my impressions. I hope to God some of those impressions are mistaken. But we shall only know when she is found and everything thrashed out in the open. Pray God I'm not making things worse for her.'

Harton turned and faced the inspector. He was rubbing the tops of the fingers of his right hand into the palm of the left and watching the action as if expecting something to come of it. Purbright waited silently.

'I've told you that I knew about Julia and Tring – well, knew half and guessed half. You can imagine that hearing at work last Monday about his getting killed in that accident came as a bit of a shock. Later on, I thought about it and read what there was in the paper. I suppose I ought to have felt some sort of satisfaction, but I didn't. Things didn't feel right. I kept on watching Julia for signs of reaction, but instead of looking upset she seemed actually calmer than usual. Then, all of a sudden, she wasn't there any more. From that moment I was really scared. And why? – Because it was then that I admitted to myself the possibility I'd been afraid to recognise immediately after the accident.'

'Which was, sir?'

'That Julia had had something to do with it.'

'With the accident?'

Harton nodded. 'I was awake nearly all the night, wondering and worrying, but it wasn't until the next day – last night, actually, as I told you – that I came across that motor-cycling kit. And after that, the picture, that filthy bloody picture. From then on, I tried not to think. I just rang Chubb and waited for somebody to come.'

Purbright replaced in the drawer the two tubes.

'I'm sure you've acted for the best in the circumstances, Mr Harton. I appreciate what a strain this business must be. What I propose to do now is this. I shall ask my sergeant to await me at headquarters. Then, with your permission, we shall come back here again as soon as possible after lunch and take a thorough look round the house. We can also use the opportunity to ask you a few more questions and perhaps take your formal statement.'

Harton seemed to be only half aware of Purbright's words. He stared in front of him for two or three seconds, then gave a start. 'Yes, sure, of course . . .' He looked round the room, saw the phone as if for the first time, and waved towards it.

'Thank you, sir.'

Sergeant Love, Purbright reflected as he picked up the phone, was not going to be pleased. He had planned, with that abiding childlike confidence in the inviolability of sporting fixtures which made him one with Drake, to travel to Peterborough that afternoon as a co-opted member of the Flaxborough Furnishing Company's mixed hockey club, for which his young lady played goal.

Chapter Thirteen

BEFORE THAT SATURDAY WAS OVER, THE IMMEDIATE enjoyment prospects of more officers than Sergeant Love were dashed. On Purbright's urgent application, Mr Chubb agreed that every CID man who could be reached either on or off duty, should be mobilised, together with three or four uniformed constables.

Their tasks, consisting of nothing more dramatic than walking about and asking much the same questions over and over again, had four main objects: to bring to a conclusion the inquiry already instigated into the local provenance of Glenmurren malt whisky; to find some person among the relatives and known acquaintances of Julia Harton who knew or could suggest her present whereabouts; to seek among the showmen, odd job men and hangers-on in the fair a more satisfactory clue to the identity of the second rider in the module 'Hermes' than had been forthcoming so far; and to speed the interrogation of counter assistants at every chemist's shop in the locality where someone might have bought recently two tubes of 'Karmz' pills for the prevention of travel sickness.

Aid on a wider, but not necessarily more productive, scale was canvassed in a message for transmission to all police forces throughout the country. This asked that Mrs Julia Harton, aged 31, housewife, of number six, Oakland, Flaxborough, who might have registered at an hotel on or subsequent to September 11, be detained for questioning in relation to the death of a man in a fairground at Flaxborough on September 6. The picture circulated was a wedding portrait by Spoongate Studio, Flaxborough, and not, Purbright thought, much of a current likeness, but he had firmly vetoed Love's suggestion that a more lively response to their appeal would be secured by the circulation of copies of the other photograph in their possession.

First result of the local campaign of inquiry was achieved in less than an hour. The officer responsible was P.C. Hessle. In the second pharmacy he entered, a shop on East Street, he found a girl who remembered very well selling two packs of 'Karmz' the previous week. The double sale was what impressed the occasion on her mind; it was the normal thing to buy one pack only – well, they weren't sweets, were they?

P.C. Hessle, overwhelmingly conscious of the gravity of his mission, forbore from trading opinions. He demanded instead an effort to recall the age, sex, and physical characteristics of the party who had made the purchase.

'Well, it was this bird in motor-cycle get-up, wasn't it?' replied the girl, in that curiously rhetorical tone of disdain that implied the questioner to be an ageing mental defective.

'I'm asking *you*, Miss,' said Mr Hessle, icily.

'And I'm telling you, aren't I? Of course, it could have been a feller. You can't tell, can you?'

Pressed for less equivocal details, the girl conferred with the shop manager and then told the policeman that yes, it *was* last week – on the Thursday morning, actually – and it must have been a bird because she spoke, well, a bit posh, sort of, but nobody could be sure, not with that great skid-lid hiding half her face.

P.C. Hessle's finding, such as it was, proved an isolated success. None of the 'Moon Shot' operators could add to what they had told both police and insurance men already, which was simply that apart from noticing a number of motor-cyclists among the customers (a not unusual circumstance) they had seen nothing memorable in the way of faces or behaviour on the night of the accident.

The two plain clothes men entrusted with the straightforward but substantial labour of visiting every one of the forty-three innkeepers of Flaxborough and the manager of every shop and off-licence where spirits were sold, had worked by closing time about two-thirds of the way through their list. They had found no one who could recall having stocked Glenmurren whisky within the past ten years or even having been asked for it. It was, the more knowledgeable declared, a very pricey liquor and not often encountered in these hard times.

Perhaps the most discouraging outcome of the day's work was the discovery that Julia Harton's sole surviving near relative, her father, Mr Clay, headmaster of Flaxborough Grammar School, was not only ignorant of his daughter's disappearance but resolved to treat it with the utmost scepticism until the police could prove to his satisfaction that she was not making a melodramatic gesture in the hope of discrediting him, Mr Clay, 'in the eyes of my boys'.

It was Sergeant Love who had gone directly from the Hartons' home to interview Mr Clay at the house on Field Street still known by its eighteenth-century name of the Headmaster's Lodging.

'Do you mean you think Mrs Harton may have gone off just to annoy you?' he asked.

'I wouldn't say that, exactly,' replied Mr Clay. He rubbed his nose, as if to impart an even higher polish to it, which would not have been easy, for every feature between Mr Clay's stiff white linen collar and the first ledger-line of his thin but strictly distributed hair was as shiny as glazed porcelain. 'No, no – not to annoy me.'

'Why, then?' persisted Love.

'Why does any young person in these times do anything?

To express what he or she supposes to be freedom from obligation and independence of authority. A passing phase, one hopes.'

'Your daughter's a bit of a campus rebel, is she?' inquired the sergeant, good-naturedly desirous of showing himself familiar with the phraseology of higher education.

Mr Clay looked strongly inclined to put Love in detention, but asked instead if it was 'that husband of hers' who had taken the story of disappearance to the police.

'Mr Harton telephoned us yesterday.'

'Mm,' said Mr Clay, pursing his lips so that his cheeks looked shinier than ever. Then, with sudden end-of-interview resolution, he strode to the street door, opened it and bade Love a good afternoon.

As the sergeant walked from the Lodging, he would not have been surprised to hear Mr Clay call out: 'Next boy!'

The police station that evening presented to such pedestrians as still were about in Fen Street the sight of an unusual number of lighted windows, associated, it seemed, with the presence at the roadside of several cars and the occasional arrival or departure of men who looked as if they had been on their feet all day.

Among the cars was the chief constable's Daimler. Mr Chubb, anxious to subscribe to the principle of equality of sacrifice, had closed his greenhouse, noted that it was a poor night on television, and deputed to Mrs Chubb the feeding of the dogs. He then had looked in at his club for an hour or so and was now, at a little before nine o'clock, asking Love in the front office if Mr Purbright was still in the building.

'The inspector's in the murder room,' Love declared.

Mr Chubb stared at him in alarm. 'The *what*?'

'In the CID office,' the sergeant amended.

The chief constable found Purbright and two detectives seated at the big central table. One of the detectives was screwing some sheets of newspaper into a ball. Purbright was wiping his hands on his handkerchief. There was a smell of fried fish.

'Ah – a little ad hoc nourishment, gentlemen?' Mr Chubb donned a democratic smile. It put Purbright in mind of toothache, bravely endured.

The two detectives murmured something about 'pressing on' and went out with their ball of fish and chip wrappings.

'And how are things going, Mr Purbright?' Mr Chubb placed a pair of yellow pigskin gloves inside the slightly raffish county cap that he wore as a sign of off-duty diligence. The cap he set on the top of a filing cabinet, beside which he remained, leaning lightly back against it, hands clasped behind.

Purbright gave him first a summary of the interview with Harton.

Mr Chubb listened, as he always did, with courtesy and every sign of attention. But then he frowned dubiously.

'Rather bizarre goings on, I should have thought, Mr Purbright. I know odd things happen nowadays even in the nicest districts, but the liaison alleged by this man sounds right out of character.'

'Do you know Mrs Harton, sir?'

Mr Chubb blew upon some imaginary porridge. 'Not to say *know* her exactly.' He perked up one eyebrow. 'Of course, you know who her father is?'

'Clay. Headmaster at the Grammar School'.

'Not very nice for him,' said Mr Chubb, ruminatively.

The inspector said no, he supposed it wasn't. Then he handed to the chief constable the photograph that had been found in the dressing-table drawer at Oakland.

Four or five seconds went by.

'Goodness gracious me!' breathed Mr Chubb at last. He gave the picture further scrutiny, holding it for a while upside down.

When he finally handed it back, it was with a slow shake of the head.

'I simply do not understand,' he said, 'how a young woman

of good family and decent schooling, who has married well and lives in a beautiful house, could sink to behaviour like this. I sometimes am tempted to despair of human nature, Mr Purbright, I really am.'

The inspector said: 'The implication of a blackmail attempt is very strong, sir. That message could mean nothing else. So Mrs Harton's reaction – assuming that she did engineer the death of her lover – might almost be construed as a reason for you not to feel too pessimistic.'

Mr Chubb frowned. 'I don't quite see what you mean.'

'Well, sir, she must have been sensitive to the value of her respectability, after all. Otherwise, she would not have sought to protect it.'

Mr Chubb was a far from unintelligent man. But in his long and, on the whole, amicable relationship with his detective inspector, he had never been able to decide to his own satisfaction whether Purbright's observations were intended to flatter or to bewilder him. He therefore had evolved a specially pliable defensive shield which could take, as seemed apposite at the moment, the shape of wisdom absolute, of a democratic willingness to learn, of the remembrance of an important engagement elsewhere, or even of a good-humoured and altogether spurious stupidity.

On this particular occasion, still winded perhaps by what he had just seen, he contented himself with: 'Be that as it may, Mr Purbright,' and asked what progress there had been towards tracing Mrs Harton.

'None so far, sir. She has some distant relations in the West Country, according to her husband, but he thinks they are virtually strangers so far as she is concerned. Such friends as we have been able to interview up to now profess themselves completely ignorant.'

'Why should she have taken it into her head to run away when she did, instead of straight away after that fellow's death? She waited four or five days.'

'I put that point to her husband, sir. He believes she went off with a man. But of course he's been seeing lovers under the bed ever since he found that photograph. Her having waited for some specific acquaintance – accomplice, even – might explain the delay in leaving. I'm not convinced, though.'

'You're not?'

'No, sir. There was no reason, so far as she could have known, to run off. Her association with Tring had been kept reasonably secret. She had gone to a lot of trouble to disguise herself as just another motor-cycling pal of his. And there was a very fair chance that the coroner would record a misadventure verdict. The most likely explanation is that she panicked because of something she learned that evening at her husband's works. There may even have been a row; he'd not admit it, of course. He says he didn't actually see his wife when she came to the factory.'

'She must have gone for some purpose, though.'

'You would think so, wouldn't you.'

'Tell me, Mr Purbright' – the chief constable shifted his position slightly – 'what do you make of this tale that's going around the club tonight?'

Purbright knew that Mr Chubb would not make such a crassly enigmatic reference just to annoy him or to sustain some sort of 'old buffer' act. It was a sign of his being worried about something. Purbright patiently awaited enlightenment.

'It is being suggested,' said Mr Chubb, very carefully, 'that . . . no, no, not suggested – hinted – it is being hinted that Mrs Harton has not left Flaxborough at all. That she is still – you take my point, don't you? – still at her husband's factory. In, ah, one form or another.' And the chief constable looked down at his impeccably polished brogues with an expression of grave distaste.

'A very attractive theory,' said the inspector, with a cheerfulness that earned him a sharp glance from Mr Chubb, 'and one that was bound to be put forward sooner or later, bearing in mind the nature of the factory's product.'

'You don't think there might be something in it?'

'No, sir. Not unless Harton is incredibly devious – and lucky enough to have had what they call the ingredient intake section of the plant to himself long enough to butcher his wife – and I'm afraid I mean that literally, sir, in this context – clean up, and dispose of clothing and so on. The machinery is very sophisticated, apparently. It rejects manufactured substances such as cloth and also anything harder than bone – teeth, for instance, and metal objects.'

Mr Chubb looked impressed. 'You're extremely well-informed, Mr Purbright.'

'I thought it would do no harm to learn something of the mechanics of the thing. Harton's works manager was at the plant when I went to look round earlier this afternoon. He was very helpful. He was also insistent that there is a rule that the intake section should never be unattended while the machinery is running, so that would seem to preclude any attempt by Harton to dispose of a body. Incidentally, it was at the intake that Tring used to be employed.'

'Indeed,' said the chief constable. He turned and retrieved his cap and gloves. 'Should you require any further help, Mr Purbright. . . .'

'That is very generous of you, sir, but I propose to run the thing down now until tomorrow. Our main hope of a development lies in efforts which doubtless are being made elsewhere to find our fugitive. There should be a story of sorts in some of the papers tomorrow. The Press is a great turner over of stones.'

Purbright's confidence proved not to be misplaced. No fewer than five national Sunday newspapers carried accounts the following morning. They ranged from the *Express*'s concern for a missing heiress to the revelation in the *Graphic* that a fun-loving housewife was being sought by the police following the death of a local Hell's Angel in a Tunnel of Love.

Perhaps the most intriguing suggestion was that offered by the *Empire News*, which argued from the presence in Flaxborough of a travelling fair that Julia Harton was likely to have become involved in 'a raggle-taggle gypsy-type elopement situation'.

The *Dispatch* contented itself with an almost unexpanded version of the official police circular. And somehow it was more chilling to learn simply that Julia Harton, aged 31, married woman, was thought able to help the police in connection with the death of a young man on September 6th, than to be treated to the high-pitched speculation of more enterprising journals.

The paper which Hugo Rothermere succeeded in borrowing ('I've just flown in from Ankara – would you mind?') from a fellow customer in a Camden Town coffee bar, happened to be the *Dispatch*. Mr Rothermere's idle survey of the news pages was brought to a sudden halt by his catching sight of a youthful Julia, waxenly demure in bridal headdress, below the headline: 'Missing After Fairground Death Mystery.'

He stared. The picture had the flat unreality, the curiously posthumous-seeming air of any studio portrait transferred to newsprint. It looked, he thought, sinister.

Mr Rothermere read and re-read the accompanying text. The owner of the paper got down from his stool and shuffled around a little to indicate his desire to depart. Wordlessly, Mr Rothermere handed back his property and stared past him at the wall.

For twenty minutes, Mr Rothermere morosely sipped at three consecutive cups of coffee. No one else entered the bar. The proprietor, a plump, bald-headed Lithuanian in shirt and trousers, whose main object in opening on a Sunday morning was to polish his urns in peace, glanced occasionally at the sad, preoccupied gentleman with the meticulously groomed whiskers and boulevardier's hat, and wondered if he were an émigré nobleman, lamenting old days in Petersburg.

At last the nobleman roused himself and asked if he might use the establishment's telephone. He had the look of one who had reached a difficult decision.

Sure, said the proprietor – right there at the end, by the pin table. He as nearly as dammit added 'Your Excellency'.

Mr Rothermere dialled directory inquiries and requested the number of a Miss Lucilla Teatime, of Flaxborough. No, he did not remember the address, but he supposed that the duplication within one town of such a name as Teatime was very unlikely.

In less than a minute he was dialling again.

A woman's voice answered. It was pleasant, carefully modulated, almost musical. Musical and, oddly enough, accompanied by harmonious sounds. Mr Rothermere listened intently for a moment before he spoke. Of course, bells. He remembered those Flaxborough bells.

'Lucy!' He made the word sound like a celebration.

'Who is that?'

'Oh, come now. Don't you know?'

Recognition warmed the reply. 'Good heavens . . . Mortimer!'

'Well, yes and no. Mortimer, yes. But this is one of my Rothermere periods.'

'I shall try and remember.'

'Lovely to hear you, Lucy.'

'You too, Mortimer.'

The exchange of pleasantries exhausted in a remarkably short time the first of the pair of tenpenny pieces that Mr Rothermere had set in readiness on the coin box. He inserted the second and swept straight to the point.

'My dear, I have been most shamefully betrayed by an organisation that hired my professional services. I cannot particularise at the moment, but you doubtless will be distressed to learn that a perfectly innocent young woman has been involved. If you will advise – nay, if you will help . . .'

Miss Teatime's interruption was amiable, but firm. 'You mean, I presume, that she is pregnant.'

'Pregnant? Who? Good God, no – nothing like that. Much, much more serious. I can't tell you here. But it does all centre on Flaxborough and I'm sure you can help. Will you be at home this afternoon?'

Miss Teatime said that she would.

'You are near the church, I believe.'

'I am almost *in* it. The address is number five, the Close.'

'Good. I shall park unobstrusively amidst the vehicles of the faithful and come straight across. It will save awkwardness all round if my presence in the town is unremarked.'

Chapter Fourteen

JULIA HARTON WENT FOR A WALK ALONG THE SEA-front. She thought about her husband and tried to imagine his increasing bewilderment and annoyance. David could never find even a handkerchief on his own initiative; what on earth would he make of a missing wife? All she could conjure, though, was the look of confident, spoiled-child amusement that he invariably assumed whenever she voiced an opinion divergent from his own. The more annoyed he was, the more case-hardened became that armour of charm. Sometimes, she thought, she had divined behind it something other than mere wilfulness and spite – something really dangerous.

Perhaps it was this reflection and not the cool off-sea wind that dissuaded Julia from walking as far as she had intended. She climbed up from the shore and entered the more sheltered streets of the town. Before returning to the hotel, she bought a *Sunday Times*; its bulkiness seemed somehow to justify her otherwise unsatisfactory excursion.

She went into the residents' lounge. Mrs Cartwright abruptly deserted the elderly clergyman and asked her if she would like a nice cup of coffee. Yes, conceded Julia unthinkingly, she would. She began to turn the pages of the *Sunday Times* colour supplement. Five minutes passed.

'Made with all milk,' confided Mrs Cartwright, 'and with just a pinch of salt to bring out the flavour. We don't do it for everybody.'

Julia thanked her warmly; she had felt in need of a little friendliness. She tried not to look at the coffee. It was grey and had strands of boiled milk in it. She's knitted it, Julia thought. The taste was terrible.

'All right?' asked Mrs Cartwright, looking eager to have her head patted.

'Out of this world!' declared Julia, with absolute sincerity.

She had finished the coffee and was feeling somewhat queasy by the time she came across her own name in the lower half of one of the news pages.

It was an unnerving discovery, not very different from one of the dreams she had from time to time in which she found herself strolling half naked through a crowded store, except that a dream – even the most strikingly circumstantial – always had a flicker of impending wakefulness round its edges. There was no chance of this being anything but what it appeared to be: a simple square of plain type announcing a plain fact.

Plain, certainly, but wrong. It was the wrongness that scared her, and much, much more than she had ever been scared by the chimerical predicament of semi-nudity in Woolworths.

Julia read the paragraph three times, slowly and with careful attention to every phrase. She could extract nothing to lessen her dismay.

What in God's name had Mortimer been thinking of? It must have been he who had engineered the publicity. He had told her about his Fleet Street contacts, about the tiresome but useful 'working breakfasts' with the editor of the *Sunday Times*. But the pressure his agency commanded was not to be applied – or so she had understood – unless and until David refused to consider a reasonable settlement. Why had he not been given time?

There were other odd things about this newspaper report, things that not only were puzzling but had a ring of menace.

The police, it said, were 'seeking' her. Well, yes; so they were, in a sense. She was missing, presumably murdered by her husband. So they were seeking her body. Then why was their search described in this story as 'country-wide'? It sounded as if the police believed her to be mobile, to be still alive. You might search a house for a corpse, or dig up a field or two, but surely you didn't look for it all over the country?

No mention of David. Again, very odd. Was he under arrest already? No, that surely would have been stated. But at least he must have been questioned as the one and only suspect. Nothing here, though, about 'a man helping the police with their inquiries'. That's what the husband was often called until an actual charge was made.

Queerest of all, and somehow the most frightening, was this mention of the accident in the fair. What the hell was that supposed to have to do with her?

Once again, Julia looked at the lines before her. '. . . wanted for questioning . . .' Hey, how could they question a body? She hadn't noticed that before. It was *she* they wanted to question, not David. God, Mortimer really *had* ballsed it up.

And that fellow in the fair. He was just something in reserve, a name picked at random to fit the invented lover of hers who was supposed to have driven her husband mad with jealousy. It was a piece of fantasy dreamed up by Mortimer and shared by nobody else.

Or so she had believed. Now the man in the fair was the concern of the police. She, too. The police were actually looking for her, hunting *her*. Everything had gone wrong. And somewhere there in comfortable, dozy old Flaxborough, David was sitting, smug and untouched, not being sought, not being questioned.

Julia folded the *Sunday Times* and pushed it close beside her in the chair, obedient to a childish instinct to preserve her shame from questing eyes. Only when Major Cartwright came through the room a few moments later on his way to the kitchen and wished her good morning as Mrs Rothermere did she remember that Julia Harton did not exist as far as her present companions were concerned.

'In for lunch?' inquired Major Cartwright, leaning over her like an insecure scaffold pole.

'Yes. Oh, yes. Certainly.'

'Lamb,' he said. 'Cooked in Mrs Cartwright's special way. Yum yum.' He straightened and marched out.

Julia went to the box of mahogany and cut glass panels that housed the telephone. In her handbag was the diary in which she had pencilled the number given her by Mortimer. His Hampstead flat. Ring if worried or in trouble. Any time. She was worried now. She dialled carefully, moistening her upper lip with the tip of her tongue.

The telephone at the far end rang eight times. Then a voice, a woman's voice, Julia thought, answered. The voice said that it spoke from the George the Fourth public house.

Public house? Odd. 'May I speak to Mr Rothermere, please?' Perhaps the flat was attached. Upstairs or something.

'Who?'

'Mr Rothermere. Mr Mortimer Rothermere.'

'Is he a customer, dear? We're not open yet.'

'He's got a flat.'

'This is a pub, dear. No flats. P'raps you've got a wrong number.'

Julia read out what she thought she had dialled. 'That's right, dear,' said the voice. 'But we're a pub. No flats.'

'Sorry,' said Julia. She put the phone down.

Leaning back, she closed her eyes and tried to remember the address Mortimer had entered in the registration book (she would look very silly if she asked the Cartwrights if she might look it up). Something-or-other Lodge – that would be the name of the block of flats. And the street? Oil came to mind for some reason. The word oil. Olive? Oil-can ... no. Oil well ... Well Road. Of course. She dialled Directory Inquiries. Rothermere M., Well Road, Hampstead, London. Thanks.

The verdict was prompt. No telephone was listed under that name and address. Was the person a new subscriber, perhaps?

Julia said no, she didn't think so, but anyway it didn't matter.

Again she closed her eyes. There grew upon her a curious feeling that the air about her had thickened in the past half-hour and was now like jelly in which every movement was slow and laboured.

Somebody tapped the glass. Startled, Julia turned. One of the companions of the clergyman was staring in with wide, concerned eyes. 'Are you all right, dear?' the woman asked, articulating in mime in case the cabinet was soundproof.

Julia gave her a reassuring smile and raised a hand. The woman nodded and crept off towards the staircase. At once, Julia began to cry.

No, this was stupid. Self-pity she could not afford. If some sort of a trap had been sprung, with her inside it, the best course was to look for an escape hole. First, though, she had to learn the nature of the trap. What had she let herself in for? What, for God's sake, did the police think she'd done?

She put more change in readiness and dialled her father's number.

'Flaxborough double two eight nine; Headmaster's Lodging.' Clear, precise, no room for error. Good old dad. Tight-arsed as ever.

She slipped in the coin. 'This is Julia, father. Ahoy, there!' The jocularity was really the tail-end of her weeping. It held a trace of hysteria.

'Julia! Where are you? What on earth have you been up to?'

She said she was at a place on the coast in Norfolk. A small hotel. Then new doubts assailed her. Why was the old man so surprised?

'Look,' she said, 'this Rothermere character – I think he's a crook. He's skipped off.'

There was a short pause. 'Rothermere? Who is Rothermere, pray?'

'Well, he's from that Happy Endings set-up of yours, isn't he. But it looks as if he's ditched me. I mean, a false phone number doesn't inspire much confidence, does it?'

'Have you been drinking, Julia?'

'Christ! I'm worried half out of my mind and all you can do is accuse me of being drunk.'

Mr Clay's tone softened a degree. 'Not at all. I was simply asking. It has happened before, you know. And I am at a loss to understand these very odd references of yours.'

'What odd references?'

'Well, really, Julia; what am I supposed to make of talk about happy endings and people called Rothermere?'

Julia gave a long sigh, part of which came out as 'Bloody hell!'

Her father's failure to reprove this lapse into vulgarity indicated that far from being merely annoyed he was now concerned. She described briefly, with one pause to insert more money, the events of the past six days that had led to her present plight. The amatory aspect she did not mention, partly because she did not wish to overfill the cup of her father's disapproval and partly because the memory, to her surprise, quite sharply grieved her.

'You realise,' Mr Clay said quietly, when she had finished, 'that I have been visited by the police and asked questions.'

'Oh, no . . .'

'Yes. I did not know quite what to say, and I fear that I may have given the officer an impression of indifference. What I was trying to do, of course, was to make light of your leaving home lest what I felt your real reason for doing so – to escape from that lamentable marriage of yours for a couple of days – should be bandied around the town by common policemen and worse.'

What Mr Clay might consider worse than a common policeman Julia was in no mood to speculate. She asked simply what he thought she ought to do.

'Have you any money?'

'Some. Not a lot. But I've my cheque book.'

'An hotel, I feel, would be reluctant to accept a cheque from an unaccompanied lady. You had better meet your obligations in cash. And the sooner, the better.'

Julia considered. There was bloody Mortimer's share of the bill, of course. She might just manage, though. 'Yes, father,' she said, without irony.

'Have you your car?'

'No. We came in Mor . . . in Rothermere's.'

'I see. In that case, I think it will be as well if I drive down and bring you back. In the meantime, it will create a favourable impression if you take the initiative and telephone the police. Tell them only that you saw the newspaper report and intend to return home at once. Answer no questions other than simple and obvious ones. I shall tell Scorpe to be ready to look after your interests.'

Justin Scorpe, doyen of Flaxborough solicitors, was considered by Mr Clay to fulfil in the sphere of litigation a role analogous to that of the grammar school gates in the sphere of education: he effectively insulated the worth-while and the privileged from the rough-and-tumble world of the envious, the vicious and the undeserving.

'And now,' said Mr Clay, 'perhaps you will tell me as clearly as you can how I best may reach the, ah, establishment in which you are lodged.'

Chapter Fifteen

'LUCY, MY DEAR, I ENVY YOU. I TRULY ENVY YOU. THERE is nothing more comforting to the bruised spirit than Gothic glimpsed through green.'

Mr Rothermere, stretched at full length within a chintz-frilled armchair, gazed dreamily through the big window with its many small panes. The parish church of Saint Lawrence loomed only fifty yards away, across the closely mown lawn that once had been its graveyard. Two immense yew trees screened much of the lower fabric, but the tower rose stark and splendid against the afternoon sky of autumn.

He was speaking to a woman of perhaps forty-five, perhaps sixty, who looked as if she had always had her own teeth and her own bank account. Her bearing bespoke discrimination but not fussiness; her clothes testified to taste which had no need to refer to fashion more often than every ten years or so. She had the face of a listener. A certain tone, a sort of controlled vivaciousness, about her body suggested appetites healthily unimpaired. She had remarkably good legs. Her name was Miss Teatime, Lucilla Edith Cavell Teatime, and such was her character that it had never got her down.

'Your spirit would not need comforting,' said Miss Teatime, 'if you had continued to follow honest employment instead of prostituting your gifts on behalf of big business.'

'The life of a private detective is not only squalid,' replied Mr Rothermere, 'it is dreadfully insecure. Security is important to one who has misspent his youth.'

'How long have you been misspending your youth, Mortimer?'

'About fifty years. Yes, but Cultox do have this marvellous pension scheme. The time is coming when I shall want a retreat. Something monastic. I think I have a latent spirituality.'

Miss Teatime rose, as if prompted by a reminder, and went to a small, bow-fronted corner cabinet. She returned with glasses and a half-bottle of whisky.

'I liked Hive much better than Rothermere,' she said. 'It sounds villainous and suits the beard. How long have you had that, by the way?'

'Since August, last year.' Mr Rothermere accepted a filled glass, pledged Miss Teatime's health, and sampled the liquor with knowledgeable nods and grunts.

'Cultox,' he resumed, 'sent me to Brussels to pick up a little information about the Italian vintage expectations. Cultox have a process to make Chianti from methane (for God's sake keep that to yourself) and they wanted to know where to hit the market. So there I was in Brussels – an Italian count!' And Mr Rothermere grinned a grin *bolognese* and swallowed some more whisky.

Soon, though, he was looking dejected again.

'Lucy, I'm bloody worried. I really am.'

'Very well. Tell me all about it.' Miss Teatime set down her glass, selected a small cigar from a box on the table beside her, and lit it after piercing the end with a pearl-headed hatpin which she seemed to keep for the purpose.

As a prelude, Mr Rothermere drew an envelope from an inside breast pocket and let it rest, unopened, in his left hand.

'This,' he said, 'is a little mystery which I think is at the centre of this awful business that I've let myself in for. You can see it for yourself later. I'll tell you what I know first – such as it is.

'Cultox have something they call their Security Division – Christ, yes, I know – I mean, who doesn't these days? – and that is the set-up for which I work. Odd, how one's past catches up: it must have been that Duke of Windsor business that gave them a cross-reference to me . . .'

'Mortimer!'

He stopped in mid-exposition, one hand aloft.

Miss Teatime frowned fondly. 'This is Lucy – remember? Erstwhile associate in the Gentlefolk's Gold Brick Promotion Society, of Hallam Street, West. No spiels, dear lad, I beg you.'

Mr Rothermere looked innocently surprised, then subsided more deeply into his chair. Within his moustache lurked a little smile of gratification.

'You will remember,' he said, 'my Happy Endings agency?'

'I do, indeed. Marriage counselling in reverse, was it not; an ingenious enterprise.'

'One tried to ease the path of true divorce. Anyway, Cultox obviously remembered it. I was asked to come to Flaxborough and apply the old technique to a little local problem, as Sir Malcolm termed it – Malky Eisenbach, that is – he's the chairman of Cultox UK – delightful fellow and the third biggest crook in England.'

Miss Teatime nodded in instant recognition. 'One of nature's gentlemen. He's vice-president of one of my doggier charities.'

'The problem in question,' Mr Rothermere went on, 'concerned the good name of a subsidiary company which contributes a disproportionately large slice of profit to the Cultox loot. Northern Nutritionals – you know it?'

'Certainly I do. It is a factory beyond Northgate, on the Brocklestone Road, and it is the source of a delicacy called WOOF.'

'The caviare of the canine world.' Suddenly he frowned and shook his head. 'I'm sorry, Lucy. Fatuousness is an occupational disease among Cultox employees. But, dear God! We work for people who actually believe their own advertising. Our nerves are pretty taut.'

Miss Teatime uncorked the whisky. 'Take your time, Mortimer. Then when you have finished what you have to tell me, you may care to listen a while to the evening service. The organ drifts across very prettily when there is no wind.'

Mr Rothermere said that he would enjoy that, as it would

remind him of the days when he annotated Bach scores for Schweitzer. Ah yes, good old Albert, said Miss Teatime. Mr Rothermere smoothly returned to the subject in hand.

'Of course, you know what these incredible corporations are, Lucy. They try and offset their predatory commercialism with a sort of happy families ethos, especially on the managerial level. My own theory is that it's a relic of the terrible personal puritanism of the old-time moneymakers. Carnegie – you know?' He shuddered.

'Anyway, the Cultox Corporation backs up its code of moral spotlessness by using the spy network that is euphemistically described as its Security Division to report on the private lives of all Cultox executives.

'Now, then. This man Harton and his wife score very badly indeed. Incidentally, do you know them?' Miss Teatime said, yes, but not well. 'Up to the ears in turpitude,' declared Mr Rothermere, 'and a grave potential risk to the WOOF image. Or so' – he paused significantly – 'I am told when I am sent up here in my capacity of expert divorce fixer.'

Miss Teatime looked up from contemplation of her cigar. 'But would not a divorce expose the company to even further embarrassment?'

'Not if it were undefended and consequently unpublicised. You could say that clean fission is my speciality – no fallout.' Mr Rothermere juddered in a silent chuckle and gave each side of his moustache a quick little stroke. But quickly his amusement faded.

'An academic point, anyway, Lucy. No divorce was ever in prospect, as far as my wretched employers were concerned. I have been sacrificed on the altar of commercial expediency.'

'No Happy Ending?'

'This is not a matter for amusement, Lucy. We are in very serious trouble with the police. And I mean serious.'

'We?' Miss Teatime looked startled.

'Julia Harton is, certainly. And I might easily be involved as well. In any case . . .' He paused and fingered his beard, dubiously this time. 'In any case, I have a certain responsibility.'

'Yes?' Miss Teatime thought she had never seen him look so crestfallen. She hoped it was not due to the proximity of the church: the sound of hymns did depress some people quite alarmingly.

'I fear,' said Mr Rothermere with a sigh, 'that I have been unaccountably naïve.'

And he told her of the plan, formed in consultation with Harton and with Cultox Security, to break Julia Harton's stubborn opposition to an agreed divorce by baiting the trap of self-compromise with promise of a huge cash settlement; of the invention of a motor-cycling lover; of the planted clothing; of the photograph ('Maisie and Ted sent you their love, by the way'); and of the final devastating, incredible invocation of the police – presumably by Harton himself – and the suggestion in the newspapers that the man supposedly picked at random as Julia's fictional lover had died in a manner of which she had knowledge.

Miss Teatime, who had listened with such close attention that there now was nearly an inch of ash on her cigar, remained silent for several seconds more, then shook her head sadly.

'Oh, dear, Mortimer; why ever did you lend your simple talents to furthering the skulduggery of big business? You realise now, of course, where you will stand if ever your share in this affair becomes known?'

Rothermere made cheek-puffing affectation of indifference, but not convincingly.

'Unless my reading of the situation is woefully awry,' said Miss Teatime, 'you have succeeded in becoming – wittingly or unwittingly – an accessory to murder.'

The face of Mr Rothermere contorted and twitched, as if he had been asked a terribly difficult question.

Miss Teatime tossed him a crumb of reassurance. 'Accessory

after the fact,' she said. She considered further. 'Unless, of course, it is decided that you merely conspired to pervert the course of justice.'

'Now look, Lucy, this is nothing to joke about.'

'I am not joking, Mortimer. You have been extremely foolish. The fact must be faced that these people have manipulated you into a position only fractionally less dangerous than that in which you have helped to place the unfortunate Mrs Harton.'

'You might give me credit for having been reasonably circumspect. I really don't see how I can be connected with whatever Julia is suspected of doing. No address, no phone number, and Rothermere I haven't used for ages.'

'You said that you had introduced yourself to her by letter.'

'I got her to give me that back.' He looked suddenly pleased with himself.

'But you were seen in the woman's company in a restaurant, then at an hotel . . .'

'*Motel*,' Mr Rothermere corrected, as if to imply that so outlandish an indulgence did not count.

'Very well – motel. But you will allow me that the third stage of your odyssey was an hotel – the place in Norfolk.'

'True.'

'Very well, then. You have been fairly liberally exposed. Then there is the matter of your motor car. It is not exactly unnoticeable. And it doubtless bears a number. You do not seem to realise, Mortimer, that if a murder *has* been committed, the ensuing investigation will not be confined to a couple of offhand questions by a constable on a bicycle. There will be unleashed a multitude of inquisitors, photographers, fingerprint seekers . . .'

'Lucy, I do get the drift of your argument. I'm sorry, but I didn't come all the way up here to be harrowed. A little help was what I had in mind, if that is not too presumptuous.'

She smiled. 'That is better. You are sometimes too self-confident for your own good, Mortimer. Now let me see what you have in that intriguing package.'

Mr Rothermere handed over his envelope.

From it, Miss Teatime drew a metal frame within which was a photograph covered by glass.

'Careful – the back is loose,' warned Mr Rothermere. 'Look inside.'

She turned the frame over and lifted out the backing of heavy card. Beneath was a pad of tissue paper. This, too, she removed, exposing the back of the photograph itself.

On this, there were four things to be seen.

The first was a row of nine numerals, set down with a leaky ballpoint pen in the laboured style of someone unaccustomed to writing.

Immediately beneath it was a number of only four figures.

Then came a metal disc, rather more than an inch in diameter, held in place by two strips of transparent adhesive tape.

Finally, near the bottom, a further inscription in the leaky ballpoint. The letters R.I.P., followed, in brackets, by three words. *Ressicled injenius protene.*

'What, do you suppose,' Miss Teatime asked, 'is "ressicled"?'

'God knows.'

'He does not mean testicled, does he?'

'I doubt it,' said Mr Rothermere.

She studied the three words a little longer.

'P-r-o-t-e-n-e . . . that can only be protein.'

'Testicles are extremely rich in protein,' offered Mr Rothermere, helpfully.

'This middle word, I take to be either "ingenious" or "ingenuous", but the difficulty is not simply one of spelling. Neither makes sense in relation to protein.'

'None of it makes sense in relation to anything. You are on the wrong track, Lucy. What you have there is quite clearly a code. If only you weren't quite so remote out here – there's a chap at the Foreign Office I have lunch with occasionally . . .'

'Mortimer, I had the impression that it was *me* from whom you had hoped to obtain help.'

He struck his forehead, nodded emphatically, held up his hands in an attitude of contrition.

Miss Teatime reversed the photograph and looked at the young man wearing motor-cycling leathers who was half-turned from the seat in his machine to stare challengingly and with contempt at the camera.

'This is Mr Tring?'

'That is Mr Tring.'

She turned the picture over once again. 'And what is the significance of all this?'

Mr Rothermere's deflation of some moments previously was by now almost entirely corrected. He waved a hand and made little rumbles of pleasure and said ah, he believed that something extraordinary, something *quite* extraordinary, was to be deduced from what Lucy was holding.

'And why do you believe that?'

He grinned sapiently. 'Look, you have read the story of Aladdin in the *Thousand and One* (incidentally, I've a very nice edition of the Burton translation: you must borrow it some time). Abanazar, you remember, is so excited about this useless old lamp that Aladdin has the good sense not to let him have it. My employers – quite predictably – don't read books. They have allowed themselves to show excitement over Tring's possession of something they have described to me variously as a medallion, a plate, a metal disc. That' – he pointed – 'obviously is what they are after. And they are not going to get it until I know what its genie can do.'

Miss Teatime sighed and smiled. 'How pleasant it is in these barbarous times to hear a well turned literary allusion. Tell me, though, how did you come by this?'

'Oh, quite fortuitously.'

'You mean you stole it.'

'No, no. I stole the photograph. The medallion happened to be taped to the reverse side – as you can see.'

Miss Teatime indicated the first row of numerals. 'At least, there should be no mystery about this. It is a telephone number, surely, prefixed by the 01 code for London.'

Mr Rothermere nodded. 'As you say, no mystery. But a little surprise, I think. I do happen to know that it's the number of the head office of Parish-Biggs, a company of food manu-facturers second only to my employers in size and rapacity.'

The brow of Miss Teatime rose delicately. 'And what have you made of this second group of figures?'

'Nothing. I have not had time to think about it. Another telephone number, presumably.'

'There are only four digits, so the probability is that it is a local number. Were you not tempted to dial it?'

'Lucy, I have been extremely busy. In any case, what was I supposed to say when somebody answered?'

Miss Teatime did not pursue the matter, but turned her attention instead to the medallion.

She peeled back the strips of tape and examined first one side of the disc, then the other. There were several deep, irregular indentations in both surfaces, but parts of an inscrip-tion had survived. The circumference of the disc was also badly damaged, one section having been sliced away completely.

After fetching a sheet of writing paper and a magnifying glass from the bureau, Miss Teatime re-lit her cigar and began a systematic interpretation of such lettering on the medallion as was still discernible. She was watched, somewhat morosely, by Mr Rothermere, who tilted the residue of his whisky slowly from side to side of his glass in time with the hymn that reached them faintly from the choristers of Saint Lawrence's.

At the end of five minutes or so, Miss Teatime handed him the paper.

She had set down, in bright blue ink:

WINSTON C or G——— -₃ —DWELL CL—E

Mr Rothermere stared at it for some seconds. He looked up. 'Very illuminating.'

'Do you not know what this thing is?' Miss Teatime asked, holding the disc lightly between finger and thumb.

'No idea.'

'You are a poor sort of detective, Mortimer.'

'I am a tired sort of detective.'

Miss Teatime put a hand on his arm. 'It is not kind of me to tease you after all your journeyings. Especially as you have yet another return trip to make this evening.'

'Oh, God!' He had started up in his chair and was wincing, as if in pain.

'I am sorry, Mortimer, but your staying here is out of the question. Stop somewhere on the road if you wish, but you must be clear of Flaxborough as soon as possible. Leave these with me' – she set to one side the photograph, frame and medallion – 'and I shall see what they may be made to yield in the way of helpful information.'

Mr Rothermere was tenderly exploring something behind his back.

Miss Teatime looked concerned. 'Anything wrong?'

A resolute head-shake. 'Just my little Spanish souvenir.' He straightened and finished his drink.

'Sunburn?' inquired Miss Teatime.

Mr Rothermere's 'Shrapnel, actually' was almost, but not quite, too quiet to be heard.

Chapter Sixteen

JULIA HARTON'S RETURN TO FLAXBOROUGH WAS awaited that Sunday evening by two people in particular whom the Norfolk police had considered proper to advise of it. One was her husband. The other was Inspector Purbright.

The arrangement, made with the approval of Mr Clay, whose manner and calling impressed the Norfolk officers as being hallmarks of civic respectability, was that his daughter should accompany him directly to the Headmaster's Lodging where every facility would be provided for an official interrogation.

David Harton sounded on the telephone to be greatly relieved, as indeed he was, for Bobby-May had arrived just before four o'clock, insistent upon practising return volleys against the north gable of the Harton home and seemed to find utterly unintelligible his argument that a sudden call by the police, with or without his wife, would expose them to great embarrassment.

Harton went into the garden to tell her the news.

Even after nearly two hours of leaping, scurrying, swinging and intercepting, Bobby-May was as cool, and drew breath as calmly, as a mannequin.

'Oh. So Awful Julia is on the way home, is she?' Bobby-May held her racquet in the manner of a frying-pan, a tennis ball, egg-like, balanced almost motionless in the centre of the strings.

'*Her* home. Not here, fortunately.'

Suddenly, she sent the ball sailing upward and caught it effortlessly in three extended fingers of her left hand. 'I said you were fussing over nothing.'

'That inspector could still drop in. Or one of his myrmidons. Bobo, you really will have to go.'

She shrugged lightly, then thrust a hand behind his back. He felt the tennis ball being rolled up and down the line of his spine. 'I'll have to shower first,' said Bobby-May. 'Have to. I don't want to pong in church.'

'God, all right, but be as quick as you can, there's a darling.'

She looked at him with sulky speculation. 'Aren't you going to rub me down?'

146

'I do have some phone calls to make. Then I'll see. But for God's sake let's get the decks cleared, shall we?'

As they walked together into the house, Bobby-May was frowning, head down. 'Do you know ...' she began, then relapsed into silence. She dragged her racquet along the wall-paper in the hall, leaving a long indented line.

'Do I know what?' Harton, for the moment less apprehensive of awkward encounters, slipped a hand into the waistband of her tennis briefs and partially untucked the yellow, cotton T-shirt. The skin beneath was cool and absolutely dry.

'Nothing,' she said, suddenly. 'Nothing, nothing, nothing.' The long, white legs were racing away from him, halfway up the staircase already. At the first turn she halted and set down her racquet and ball. Then, quite casually, she crossed arms, bent forward, and peeled the T-shirt over her head.

Harton remained at the foot of the stairs, gazing up, bewildered. A movement distracted him; the ball had rolled off the top step and was descending, one stair at a time at first, then in ever bigger bounds until it sailed past him towards the front door.

He looked again at Bobby-May. She stood erect, legs close together and was making experimental movements with hips and shoulders whilst peering down, with chin tucked in tightly, to observe their effect on her naked breasts. 'Digger,' she remarked conversationally after a while, 'used to call them my headlamps.' She gave a couple of little hops on her heels. The breasts bounced and quivered. 'He was horribly common.'

She grinned, as if at a highly satisfactory memory, then swung about and quickly climbed the rest of the stairs.

Harton seemed inclined to follow her, but after standing irresolute for a moment he walked instead through the kitchen to a small office-like room, the door of which he shut behind him. He sat by the telephone and dialled a number.

'Charles? David Harton. Yes. Look, you asked me to keep

you in the picture developmentwise. I thought you'd like to know they've traced my wife. Yes, it *is* sooner than expected. She rang them, apparently – yes, the police. Saw something in the paper. Not to worry, though, Charles. I think everything's tied up. We'll just have to play it as it comes, won't we? Oh, and Charles – I've a shrewd notion that friend Rothermere might try and be a bit awkward. Stroppy, you know? A slight attack of ethics, by the look of it . . . Odd? But how right you are, Charles. Decidedly odd bird. Not that he can do anything now. Not without jumping right in the shit himself. Right, then, Charles, I'll be in touch if need be. Sorry, ye old what? Ye old hostelry – oh, I get you. Yes, great, great. Chow, Charles.' He put down the phone. 'Sarcastic bleeder.'

Before he had time to leave the office, there was an incoming call. It was from Inspector Purbright, who thought that Mr Harton would like to know that his wife had arrived in Flaxborough and seemed to be well. She was at present conferring with her solicitor at the home of her father, where she had expressed the desire to stay for the time being.

'You say she's well, inspector. She *is* all right, isn't she?' Relief and anxiety contested for control of Harton's voice.

'Perfectly, sir. Don't worry, we'll look after her.'

'Tell her not to worry about a thing. I'm coming over right away.'

'I don't think that would be a very good idea, sir, if you don't mind. Not just now.'

'But why? Look, you can't forbid a woman to talk to her own husband, whatever you think she might have done.'

'It is not I who am forbidding anything, Mr Harton. Your wife says she does not wish to see you. She is very firm on the point.'

'Oh,' said Harton, very quietly. 'I see.' And again, softly and with much sadness, 'I see.'

Gently, he replaced the telephone, paused, stood, strode purposefully from the room, rubbing his hands.

'Darl!' he called, from halfway up the stairs. 'It's all right. Awful Julia and her policemen won't be coming after all.'

He entered the bathroom and threw half the contents of the airing cupboard on the floor in his search for a large and suitably bright-coloured towel.

'Ready for the bunny!' he called.

The energetic splashing ceased and the sound of a rain of water droplets on plastic curtaining gradually died. There appeared in the doorway a wetly gleaming, bright pink Bobby-May, eyes averted, one hand cupped protectively round a breast, the other splayed over her groin, a starfish stranded across a weedy crevice.

He held the towel up like a cloak. She turned and waited submissively to be enwrapped. He put his arms about her and tightened them. Her warmth passed through the thick, rough cotton almost instantly. So, surprisingly, did the delineation of quite subtle details of her body – little wrist bones, a gentle corrugation of muscle above and below the cleft of the navel, the rubberiness of ribs, the unsuspected angularity of knee-caps, and that curious discrepancy in hardness that Harton had noticed before between one nipple and the other.

For a while, he moved his hands, open-palmed, as if exploring a parcel, then began taking hold of the towel here and there and scrubbing the skin beneath.

Bobby-May made a murmuring noise indicative of pleasure. Harton rubbed harder. The line of his mouth tightened, but it was still upturned at the corners. He breathed deeply, regularly, in the manner of an athlete.

The girl twisted this way and that within the towel cloak, as if to guide Harton's ministrations to especially demanding parts of her body. He had begun to vary the scrubbing with a sort of kneading technique, hooking his fingers round the flesh and levering the rigid thumbs into it with a firmness that gradually increased to a degree not far short of ferocity.

Bobby-May was leaning now at an angle against the bathroom

wall. She, too, was breathing deeply, but much more quickly than Harton. Every now and again, she stiffened into immobility for a second, then relaxed, gasping. Her eyes were closed. Her mouth was a round hole in which the tongue made spasmodic appearance like some nervous pink bird.

Harton's movements became less well co-ordinated and more brutal. He thrust a hand beneath the towel and clutched the girl's thigh in an attempt to pull her off balance. She began to slide to the wet floor. Still she did not look at him although fingers rendered vice-like by countless hours of racquet-wielding had seized the invading hand and were conveying it to her mouth. The sudden bite made Harton cry out. His voice in pain was high and petulant, like a boy's.

Only then, in response to the cry, did Bobby-May open her eyes. The corners of her mouth dimpled in a slow, sweet smile.

'You'll thank me for that, Davy, when I come to you as a bride.'

'You vicious little cow! You needn't think you can play games like that with me!' Boring one knee into her stomach, he forced her the rest of the way to the floor and tried to kneel astride her while he groped clumsily amidst the twisted towelling, seeking to pull it apart.

Bobby-May gave sign of neither distress nor alarm. She simply giggled.

'Cow! Bloody cow!' Harton punched wildly into the bundle he straddled. By ill luck, his fist connected with the point of the girl's elbow. Pain streaked up his arm like a white-hot arrow.

The giggles were renewed.

Anger and nausea confused and soon incapacitated him, but for several minutes after Bobby-May had squirmed free and leaped, laughing like a tiddly schoolgirl, beyond his reach, he continued to belabour her with repetitive obscenities.

At last he got up from the floor, having seen that threads of blood were oozing from two punctures in the back of his right hand.

He stared at the wounds, put them under the tap, and sought a bottle of disinfectant and plasters in the cabinet above the wash-basin.

Bobby-May reappeared at the door. She was dressed.

'I'm off now, Davy. Mums will be waiting to go to church.'

Harton was still examining his hand. He spoke without looking away from it. 'You murderous sodding bitch . . . I've probably got blood poisoning.'

Bobby-May's eyes widened and glistened. 'I'll make up for everything when we're married. It will be worth waiting for, Davy. It will, truly.'

'Christ, this is haemorrhaging. You bit into a sodding artery. Do you realise that?'

' 'Bye, lamb.'

He raised his head abruptly. His face was dark with fury.

Bobby-May met his wild glare with mild and patient regard. 'Poor Davy, you're all upset. It's probably the worry about Awful Julia.'

She came to him in four little running steps.

'Poor, silly Davy! Here – Bobo make better.'

Reluctantly, eyes half closed with apprehension, he let her take the hand and dry it with butterfly-light strokes of fresh cotton wool. She peeled one of the plaster strips and smoothed it over the skin. Harton started and drew a sharp intake of breath. She stood on the tips of her tennis shoes and without releasing his hand kissed him gently on the mouth. Finally, she drew the hand beneath her T-shirt and held it cupped for several seconds over first one breast, then the other.

'Better now? Advantage Davy!' She was down the stairs and opening the front door before Harton could think of anything else to say.

The boys of Flaxborough Grammar School would have been much intrigued by the nature of the gathering that Sunday evening in their headmaster's big, dingy Edwardian sitting-room. In addition to Mr Clay himself, looking even more vigilant and authoritative than usual, there were present his married, and therefore fearfully old, daughter; a solicitor with a long neck, lots of hair in his nose, and huge black spectacles that he was always taking off and putting on again; and not one, but two, policemen in plain clothes – a detective inspector and a sergeant who clawed down into a notebook everything that the others said.

Julia, on Purbright's insistence, had taken a small meal, despite her own declared disinclination to eat; and Mr Justin Scorpe had downed a couple of glasses of Mr Clay's sherry in order to help put at ease, if not the company as a whole, at least Mr Scorpe.

The inspector sat at a big oval mahogany table in the middle of the room, with Love on his left. Facing them was Julia Harton. Mr Scorpe, his long, craggy head supported on three long, bony fingers in an attitude of meditation, sat on a chair upholstered in red velvet, a little apart from his client but within leaning distance of conference with her. He looked grave and immensely wise.

Mr Clay, very upright and prim-mouthed, was seated in the background: a silent supervisor, whose presence was evidenced by the glint of glasses in the shadows.

Purbright began by putting to Julia a string of formal questions concerning age, occupation, relationships, recent movements. He was gentle in manner and seemed regretful at offering such banal fare. Then he asked: 'Were you acquainted, Mrs Harton, with a young man called Robert Digby Tring?'

'No, I wasn't.'

'I should like us to be quite clear on this point, Mrs Harton. Robert Tring was a man in his early twenties who worked in your husband's factory. People mostly called him Digger. He was a motor-cycling enthusiast. You never met him?'

'Never. Not knowingly, anyway.'

'So you can think of no circumstances in which you might

have been photographed in the company of Robert Tring?'

'You mean specifically in his company, or as two people in a crowd?'

'Specifically,' said Purbright. 'Just the pair of you.'

'As I said, I've never met the man.'

The inspector nodded, as if satisfied.

'Are you,' he asked, 'interested in motor-cycles, Mrs Harton?'

She looked perplexed. 'Certainly not. Should I be?'

Purbright's smile seemed to imply agreement that the notion was an odd one, but he asked nevertheless: 'Do you possess, or have you ever worn, the sort of clothing which motor-cyclists usually adopt?'

Julia felt a small tremor – not quite of fright, perhaps, but certainly of sharp apprehension. She tried to consider how she could most safely frame a reply, but as the moments passed it became more and more difficult to think. In the end, she had to content herself with a bald negative.

'You're happy, are you, with that answer, Mrs Harton? You did seem to be having some doubts.' Purbright's concern sounded kindly enough. It did not, however, pass the guard of pensive Mr Scorpe.

'My client,' he declared, 'is perfectly entitled to give the framing of her answers due consideration, inspector, however long that takes.'

'Oh, perfectly entitled, Mr Scorpe,' the inspector agreed. 'I was only anxious that subsequent questions of mine, touching the same matters, should not sound wilfully obtuse.'

'I don't think I quite take your point,' rumbled Mr Scorpe, sweeping off his great spectacles and peering at them, suspiciously.

'For example' – Purbright leaned down and took from the floor by his feet a loosely wrapped parcel – 'I was going to ask Mrs Harton how these articles came to be in a cupboard in her kitchen.' He disclosed the jacket, breeches and boots.

'You do see my difficulty, Mr Scorpe? In view of her last reply?'

The solicitor said nothing. He looked at Julia.

She stared sullenly at the clothing, said she had never seen it before, and asked why she should take the inspector's word for its having been found in her kitchen.

'Do you travel much, Mrs Harton?' Purbright asked.

'No more than other people, I suppose.'

'Are you a *bad* traveller? Does it upset you?'

'No. Why?'

'About three weeks ago, did you buy two tubes of "Karmz" anti-sickness pills at Parkinsons, in East Street?'

'I did not.'

'Have you ever bought such tablets?'

'Never.'

Purbright glanced aside to see how Sergeant Love's shorthand was coping, then took an envelope from the folder before him.

'Mrs Harton, I am about to show you a photograph and to ask you some questions concerning it. If you wish your solicitor or your father to see the photograph, you must say so. At this stage, I am prepared to respect your wishes.'

Julia watched him turn the envelope over in his hand, untuck the flap and extract a print. She was pale and looked, for the first time in the interview, deeply anxious.

Purbright passed the photograph across the table, face down. Julia picked it up with a little difficulty. She made no attempt to shield it from Mr Scorpe, who was now looking at her across the top of his spectacles as if, by that means, he might render their relationship totally impervious to embarrassment.

After staring at the picture for some seconds in what Love unhesitatingly decided to be horror, Julia addressed Purbright.

'Who the hell is this supposed to be?'

The inspector leaned forward to see what she was indicating with a tremulous forefinger.

'That, to the best of my knowledge, is Robert Tring.'

Julia half opened her mouth. She shook her head, looked about her with an expression of utter bewilderment, then scowled furiously at the photograph.

'Hey, this is some kind of very sick joke. Where the hell did you get it, anyway? It's a fake, a trick. Honestly, it really is. It's a filthy bloody fake!'

Mr Clay did not for an instant shift his gaze, which was fixed upon a point about three feet above his daughter's head. He was in urgent communication with his colleague, GOD, M.A. *Let not this reach the ears of the boys, and especially not those of McCorquadale and Le Brun J.*

The inspector gently took back the print.

'The boots you are wearing – I beg your pardon – *appear* to be wearing, in the photograph have been compared very carefully with those I showed you just now,' he said. 'And there are enough points of resemblance to convince me that they are the same. Do you want to say anything about that?'

Julia stared stonily down at the table. Then she glanced at the solicitor, at her father and back to Purbright.

'Would it be all right,' she asked, 'if I had a word with Mr Scorpe in private?'

'Of course.'

The lawyer rose to his feet and followed Julia out of the room. He walked with a forward stoop and parted the tails of his long, old-fashioned black coat in order to scratch his bottom.

When they returned a few minutes later, Julia looked subdued but less distressed.

She nodded towards the parcel that still lay where Purbright had put it on the table. 'I want to tell you about those,' she said.

'They aren't mine, but I have seen them before. And I *was* wearing some of them when a photograph was taken of me.

Not the photograph you showed me. I know nothing about that. It started as a sort of a joke to annoy my husband. No, not a joke. It was part of a plan, actually. Our marriage has been pretty dreadful for a long time. I wanted – I still want – a divorce. Then when this agency wrote to me I got in touch with them and . . .'

'Agency?' the inspector interrupted.

'It calls itself "Happy Endings".'

Sergeant Love looked up, delight dawning on his face, but at once stooped again to note-taking, warned off by a flicker in Purbright's eye.

'Go on, Mrs Harton.'

'Well, the idea was for them to negotiate a reasonable settlement with my husband on my behalf. I posed for a picture as a sort of good faith guarantee – so that I shouldn't go back on the divorce once proceedings had been started.'

'If this photograph is not the one for which you posed, can you explain how the man Tring came to be on it?'

Mr Scorpe intervened. 'My client has said already, inspector, that she considers the photograph to have been faked.'

'That is so, Mr Scorpe; but she has since had a private consultation with you. I simply wondered if she might now like to modify the earlier reply.'

Julia shook her head vigorously.

'Very well,' said Purbright. 'In that case, I should like to ask you how the photograph came to be in a drawer at your home – one of the drawers of the dressing table in your bedroom – in which I am told you are in the habit of keeping personal property, and to which you possess the key.'

'Do you,' inquired Mr Scorpe majestically, 'mean to tell us, inspector, that the police searched Mrs Harton's house when she was not present and had not given permission?'

'As she had been reported missing, it does not seem altogether inconsistent to suppose that neither her presence nor her permission was available at that time, sir. Our task was to find

Mrs Harton. We looked in the first instance for anything suggestive of her whereabouts. The search was made in Mr Harton's presence and with his approval.'

Purbright, cross with himself at having been provoked into pomposity, returned his attention to Julia.

'Any idea how the picture came to be in that drawer?'

'I haven't, no.'

'You've read the message written across it?'

'Yes.'

'And does that not mean anything to you?'

'Apart from its being a threat of some kind; no, it doesn't.'

Purbright removed the lid from a shallow cardboard box. 'These things also were in the drawer we've been talking about, Mrs Harton. I don't want you to think that I'm trying to place a sinister interpretation on any of them, but a couple I really do find puzzling. The photograph for one, of course. Then there are these – the two empty "Karmz" tubes. I thought you said you had never bought such things.'

She stared in apparent perplexity. 'They must be my husband's. They certainly aren't mine.'

'If I were to tell you that Mr Harton denies any knowledge of such pills and claims never to have seen those containers before, what would you say?'

'I'd say he was a damned liar, what else?' Julia had flushed angrily and was leaning forward in her chair.

'Can you suggest how the empty tubes got into that drawer?'

Mr Scorpe was gesturing in preparation for protest, but Julia spoke first.

'Certainly I can. David put them there. Don't ask me why. Some vicious little scheme of his own, I suppose.'

'And the photograph?' prompted the inspector, quietly.

'Sure. Yes. Why not? And the bloody photograph!'

'And this?'

Purbright slid across the table towards her a small slip of paper. It was a sales receipt for £37 in respect of 'Ladys m/c

jkt, 36″ blk' and dated the previous March. The slip was headed
with the name of a Manchester firm of sports outfitters.

'Yes,' shouted Julia. 'This, too, if it was there that you found
it. And for God's sake don't ask me if I've ever seen it before.
I couldn't bloody bear it.'

There was a long silence, during which nobody seemed to
think it would be a good idea to look at anyone else. Then
quietly, confidentially almost, Purbright addressed Julia.

'I imagine you could do with a rest, Mrs Harton, so I don't
propose to ask your help any more tonight. There is, however,
one question that I must put to you before I go.'

Julia nodded weary assent, and the inspector continued:

'Will you tell me, as precisely as possible, where you were
on Saturday of last week – Saturday, the sixth of September –
between eleven o'clock and midnight.'

She considered, but not for long.

'I was in bed, inspector. In bed at home. And in the company
– most reluctantly – of my husband. Is that precise enough for
you?'

Purbright bowed his head.

'Eminently.'

Chapter Seventeen

IN HER CAPACITY AS SECRETARY AND TREASURER OF
the Flaxborough and Eastern Counties Charities Alliance, Miss
Teatime was careful to keep in her office in Saint Anne's Gate
not only a street and trade directory but a reasonably up-to-
date copy of the voters' list.

She therefore anticipated little trouble in building into a full
name and address the fragmentary inscription she had copied
from the disc bequeathed by Mr Rothermere:

The last word was easiest of all to guess for a lady whose current vocation had made her familiar with the foibles of the socially aspiring. It was – it had to be – CLOSE, a designation two points up on Gardens, at least three points superior to Avenue, and a whole astral plane above a mere Road. As for —DWELL, that clearly had started as CADWELL, for the only other Closes in Flaxborough were Church, Windsor, Harley and Twilight.

There were three householders in Cadwell Close whose name began with G: Godstone, at 2; Grant, at 17; and Gill, at 20. The only two Cs were Copley and Corrigan. They lived at 13 and 18 respectively. That 13 fitted. Copley, clearly, was the winner. Copley, Anthea Katherine, sole occupant.

Miss Teatime put away the directory and voters' list and took from the shelf a long slim book, bound in a home-made cover patterned in forget-me-knots. This contained some hundreds of names, entered in alphabetical order in her own neat script. The names were of potential subscribers to charity. Miss Teatime called the catalogue her 'soft touch list'.

She turned the pages to C. Campbell ... Carstairs ... Clasket ... ah, there it was, Copley. She had thought it would be. And the entry had a little star against it, which was her private mark to indicate pelf above the average.

Miss Teatime refreshed her memory by studying the case notes opposite Mrs Copley's name. Widowed 1963; brewery shares; married daughter Australia; three poodles: Winston, Edward and Vera Lynn; frightened of black men and Chinese; addicted to peppermint creams; telephone number 3829.

Telephone ... Miss Teatime took another look at the second, the shorter, number on the back of Robert Tring's picture, confident that it would tally with Mrs Copley's. But it did not. It was 2271. Quite different. Damn.

She dialled 2271 there and then.

It rang for nearly half a minute without response. She was

about to replace the receiver when the ringing tone ceased. No one answered. She spoke. An experimental 'Hello?' There was rustling at the other end.

'Yes?' A man's voice, slightly breathless. Not friendly.

'Who is that, please?'

'Double two seven one.'

'I mean, *who* is it?'

'I've given the number. What do you want? Who is that, anyway?'

A cagey gentleman, clearly. Miss Teatime considered rapidly. The call would produce nothing on this Hello-Hello level. A key of some kind was needed. Tring? R.I.P.? Mrs Copley? Cultox? There was no knowing. And a wrong guess could do a lot of harm, if only by putting somebody on guard.

'That is Kelsey's isn't it? The shoe shop?' She had decided to disengage.

'No, it isn't.' A click and that was that.

Miss Teatime found that the call had disturbed her a little, so she poured herself a modest medicinal dose of whisky and thought about the man who had taken so long to answer the phone. He had not said much, yet even that brief and unpromising exchange had left her with the impression that he was someone she knew.

But who?

She selected another notebook. It listed the names and telephone numbers of people in the town and locality whose professions or connections rendered them of potential use to a charitable organisation. They included chairmen of committees, bank managers, veterinary surgeons, magistrates, welfare officials and inspectors of police, income tax and slaughterhouses.

The finely tapered forefinger moved swiftly from name to name, page to page, wavering for an instant now and again, or fleetingly shifting to check a number.

About two-thirds of the way through the list, the finger

hesitated, moved back one line, and halted. She made a murmur of recognition, then frowned. Phone numbers again had failed to tally. That which appeared against the name indicated by her finger was 3944.

Of course, there was a way of making sure.

Once more, she dialled 2271. The answer came not instantly but much more quickly than before. An abrupt, suspicious 'Yes?'

At once she rang off and dialled 3944.

Ten, twenty, thirty seconds went by. The number was still ringing out. Three quarters of a minute . . .

'Good morning . . .' A pause for recovery of breath. 'Four Foot Haven, Heston Lane. May I help you?'

Silently, delicately, Miss Teatime replaced her receiver. She smiled. It was very nice, once in a way, to have a wild guess confirmed. Perhaps luck would stay with her long enough to make a visit to Mrs Copley worth while.

Miss Teatime's little sports car, the cost of which modest self-indulgence she managed to implant neatly amidst the managerial expenses of a charity devoted to the relief of greengrocers' horses, was standing in Saint Anne's Place, not many yards from her office, and close to the railings of the park. She drove out into Southgate and soon was passing the semi-villas of Gordon Road and Beatrice Avenue, where, neighbours still recalled, poor Mr Hopjoy had met his terrible end in 1962, and hence into the leafy cul-de-sac of Cadwell Close.

Number 13 was a bungalow in heavily ornate stucco, the colour of dried lavender. The front door was flanked by big bay windows. Each revealed a spread of overlapping drapes of white muslin, gathered by silk cords and tassels, which gave an impression that the house was in full sail.

Miss Teatime's ring was answered instantly by a paroxysm of barking. Winston, Edward and Vera Lynn, no doubt. No, she reminded herself; probably not Winston.

She heard a human voice, female, raised in shrill but affectionate remonstration. The barking continued unabated.

The door opened three inches or so to reveal a pair of woolly muzzles and part of the anxiously frowning face of a woman of about sixty.

Miss Teatime delivered a brisk 'Good morning, Mrs Copley,' then immediately bestowed upon the poodles a smile of almost maternal admiration and an ecstatic 'Aaahh!'

A friend forthwith, Mrs Copley opened the door fully and waited patiently for her visitor to recover the power of speech.

'I do not suppose you will remember me, Mrs Copley, but we have met, I believe, on sundry occasions. Teatime is my name and I am secretary of our little family of helpful societies here in Flaxborough.'

'Oh, of course. Do please come in.'

Miss Teatime's taking a first step past the threshold was the signal for the dogs to enter a new phase of frenzy. Barking even louder than before, they darted about in short runs, each of which culminated in a clawing leap at Miss Teatime's elegant legs.

'Aaahh! Bless them!' exclaimed Miss Teatime, a professional to her fingertips.

Mrs Copley was talking. Miss Teatime watched the words being formed. She thought they were *I'd better put the boys in the kitchen* so she nodded in rueful acceptance. Mrs Copley opened a door. The dogs shot through, nearly knocking her over. Mrs Copley followed them. Smiling back at Miss Teatime, she held aloft a can and an opener. WOOF (WITH TURKEY). Her lips were moving again. *They know, don't they? They do know.* Miss Teatime beamed and wagged her head in acknowledgment.

Later, in the cool, slightly musty, quietude of Mrs Copley's sitting-room, her visitor raised a matter of delicacy. Had not the Boys numbered three at one time? Or was her memory at fault?

Mrs Copley said no, alas, she was not mistaken: there had indeed been three. But Winston now was in the Haven.

'I am so sorry,' said Miss Teatime. Softly, 'You had to have him put to sleep?'

'He was our fourth Winston,' remarked Mrs Copley, as if the name in itself held the seeds of dissolution. Then she recalled herself. 'Oh, no; he wasn't put to sleep. He had a coronary, poor boy.'

'Good gracious,' exclaimed Miss Teatime.

'Oh, it's not unusual, apparently,' said Mrs Copley. 'Mr Leaper at the Haven said it happens a lot with the best breeds. They're so highly strung, you see. I mean, take Winston. He was a fine, big boy, but never still for an instant. Never. In fact' – she laughed – 'he was such a great roustabout – quite different from Edward and Vera Lynn in there – that he never was given his real name at all. Not Winston. No, we called him Rip. And not because of Rip Van Winkle, either! Oh, he was a terror, was Rip. Everybody misses him.'

Mrs Copley remained silent a moment in fond recall. Then she frowned.

'Everybody but my sister-in-law,' she amended.

'Your sister-in-law?'

'Ethel. She lives in Brocklestone and has migraines and ever since George passed over she's insisted on coming to stay with me for a week in the summer. It's kind of her, I suppose, but of course that *is* the time when Brocklestone gets so crowded with trippers. Anyway, Ethel was very queer and unreasonable about poor old Rip, so I used to board him at the Haven whenever she came. And that's how it happened.'

'Oh, yes?'

'Rip's coronary. It was while he was in the Haven. Last month. Mr Leaper was terribly upset. Terribly.'

'He must have been,' said Miss Teatime.

'He came over personally to tell me. I thought that was rather nice of him. You know, I could hardly believe it at first.

Well, only a few days before he'd been so lively that I'd had to help hold him while they tied his identity label on his collar. That was just until he got to his proper kennel, of course – Rip always had the same one.'

'Tell me,' said Miss Teatime, 'were you able to see poor Winston – Rip, that is – before they . . .' She left the sentence reverently incomplete.

For the first time in the interview, Mrs Copley gave sign of distress. No, she said, that had not been possible. She had asked, naturally, but only to be told that poor Rip was . . . was already . . .

'Laid to rest?' prompted her visitor.

A sniff of grief. 'Cremated,' said Mrs Copley.

After a while she recovered sufficiently to suggest refreshments and a general reunion with survivors Edward and Vera Lynn.

Miss Teatime regretfully declined. There had been reaching her for some minutes the sounds of gnawing at wood.

It did not strike Mrs Copley until much later that the lady from the Charities Alliance had forgotten to give the reason for her call.

Miss Teatime drove back into town the way she had come. Her next destination was Four Foot Haven, boarding kennels and lost pets' pound, off Heston Lane.

The fair was over. The rides and sideshows had been dismantled during the weekend, and the last of the great steam engines was panting and snorting its way over the town bridge into Northgate. Its canopy, borne aloft on six gleaming twists of brass, could be seen swaying above the mass of cars and lorries which it held to a crawl in the glutted Market Place.

Once across the bridge, Miss Teatime turned left into Burton Place and entered Heston Lane at the opposite corner.

The Four Foot Haven consisted of a small huddle of sheds

and Nissen huts within a perimeter fence. It was reached by way of a narrow track between fields at the back of the big Edwardian villas on the north side of Heston Lane.

Miss Teatime's car drew up on a patch of cinder by the most imposing of the sheds. It had WARDEN on the door, which was a little open.

She stood for a moment, gazing across the open fields. The nearest buildings were those of Twilight Close, toy-like amongst neat shrubs and hedges. To the left was something bigger, newer-looking, more stark: the brick and asbestos gable of the main bay of Northern Nutritionals.

Miss Teatime considered. No, too far. A nice idea, but really too far.

She moved to the other side of her car and looked in other directions. Ah, *that* was more promising. A shed she had not noticed before, set apart from the rest, thirty or forty yards from the fence gate. She began walking towards it.

'Hey!'

Miss Teatime halted and looked back.

In the now open doorway of the Warden's hut stood a tall, angular, loosely strung-together sort of man, lank-haired and pale, whose most immediately noticeable feature was a nose like an inflamed spike.

'You can't go over there,' the man shouted. 'That's private property.'

'My dear Mr Leaper, if I were to restrict my movements to public property, I should spend the rest of my life in police stations, town halls and lavatories. Is that what you wish for me?'

The Warden wiped his spike on his sleeve and said he hadn't noticed it was her, but over there was private all the same.

Leonard Leaper, even at the relatively early age of 35, had a lot of former about him. He was a former newspaper reporter, a former minister of religion, a former gas fitter, a former valet. Having failed from his earliest years to develop any sense of relationship between ambition and capability, he had from time to time offered himself as candidate for jobs ranging from cinema projectionist to licentiate in dental surgery, and had actually landed some of them. His self-confidence was vast, but it was based upon nothing but peasant-like simplicity of mind and the central indestructible conviction that he would one day be king of England.

Miss Teatime had decided to risk one quick audacious bid to trap this heir unapparent into an indiscretion from which he could not retreat.

She drew close, glanced about her secretively, and confided: 'Mr Leaper, a couple of R.I.P. commissions are arriving today. Do I take it that there will be' – she indicated with a nod the solitary shed – 'accommodation ready?'

The Warden's small but protuberant eyes regarded her with what she feared was blank incomprehension. Several seconds passed. Then, just when she was about to try and laugh off what she had said (and what a grim exercise, she reflected, *that* would be), Leonard Leaper spoke:

'Here,' he said, 'was that *you* on the phone this morning?'

She thought quickly. Was she to go a little further in? Or to start laughing? Audacity won.

'Yes, I'm sorry I was not able to speak freely. People kept coming in.'

Mr Leaper's manner eased slightly. It became leavened with a sort of gawky bravado. He looked Miss Teatime up and down. 'Fancy *you* being in it as well, and you on all them committees and everything.'

Miss Teatime bore this slander with fortitude. She tried to look roguish.

'Mind you,' said the Warden, 'you're unlucky. Pro tem, anyway.'

'Unlucky?'

'Well, it's stopped for now because of that slip-up and then Digger's accident and everything. Nar-poo – finish.'

166

'Oh. Indeed. Because of the slip-up. Yes, of course.' Miss Teatime nodded wisely while she devised another piece of bait. Leaper clearly was susceptible to what he believed to be criminal's argot.

'In my opinion, Mr Leaper,' she said, leaning even closer towards him, 'it was Digger's intention to blow the whistle.'

Surprise, dismay, alarm, invested Leaper's countenance in rapid succession.

'Stone me!'

He made a brief twitchy survey of the scenery, then ushered Miss Teatime into his hut.

It smelled of sacking and strong tea, but was reasonably clean. She sat, uninvited, in the old-fashioned swing chair that was the only furniture it contained other than a deal table and a couple of shelves.

Leaper propped himself up against the wall. 'Stone me!' he said again (What a curiously biblical plea, thought Miss Teatime) and then, 'Digger, eh? If anybody'd asked me, I'd have said it was that bint of his who was poison.'

'Mrs Harton?' ventured Miss Teatime.

'Nar!' exclaimed the Warden, contemptuously. 'Digger's bint. His fancy piece. That kennel maid that used to be here.'

'You did not trust the kennel maid?'

'She was creepy. She said she wanted to be a vet so as she could open up veins, and all the time she was playing at ball like some little kid.'

Miss Teatime did not need entirely to rely on pretence in order to appear keenly interested.

'You know, you really are a most perceptive observer, Mr Leaper,' she told him. 'Digger's breach of trust – his double-cross, rather – is beginning to be understandable. But, of course, you already have worked that out for yourself.'

Leaper nodded carelessly. He was doing something to his thumb-nail with a jack knife.

'What was the girl's name again? I can never remember it

for long.' Miss Teatime hoped that this bit of crude skating would not bring her to grief.

The thick ice of Leaper's self-esteem held.

Without looking up, he said: 'Lintz. Bobby-May Lintz.' His lip curled. 'Bobby-May! I ask you! Her old man's editor of the local rag.' Ex-journalist Leaper would never have referred to the *Flaxborough Citizen* in such derogatory terms had he not once applied for, and been summarily denied, the post of its assistant editor.

'It was a piece of terribly bad luck that someone should send in an animal that happened to be called Rip,' said Miss Teatime, reflectively.

'You can say that again,' muttered the Warden. 'Stone me!'

'Ah, well, Mr Leaper' – she rose – 'in the circumstances we had better call the job off.'

He shut his jack knife with some difficulty and peered anxiously at his thumb. 'Yeah. Pro tem.'

Miss Teatime was about to reach for the door, which had been standing slightly ajar, when it began to move inward of its own accord.

Two men were standing outside. One, though young, was white-haired. He looked cheerful. His companion, a pace behind, did not.

'We did knock,' said the nearer man. 'You seemed busy, though. Not to worry.' He smiled.

Leaper looked quickly from one to the other and then at Miss Teatime, as if asking her to account for them. She gave a small shake of the head.

The white-haired man appeared to understand their dilemma. 'Allow me,' he said, 'to introduce ourselves. We are executive representatives of Happy Endings Incorporated. I wonder if you now have a few moments to spare, madam and sir?'

Chapter Eighteen

THE WHITE-HAIRED MAN GLANCED QUICKLY ABOUT the hut interior and pronounced it 'fascinatingly rural'. It would not be sufficiently commodious, however, to allow them to hold the kind of conference he had in mind. Perhaps Miss Teatime could suggest somewhere else?

'I'm Charles, by the way,' he added, 'and this' – he indicated his companion, loitering diffidently in the doorway–'is Simon.'

'Of the Cultox Corporation?' inquired Miss Teatime, pleasantly.

'Of Cultox, as you say. Security division.'

The Warden was glowering. 'What was all that about happy endings and everything?'

'A little pleasantry, Mr Leaper. I fancy Miss Teatime will understand.'

She said: 'You seem to know my name, Mr Charles. Yours is not familiar to me. However, names are of no concern to our little four-footed friends, so why should they matter to us?'

'What a beautiful philosophy,' Charles declared. Simon nodded gravely in the background. His clasped hands made slow and continuous movements, like a stomach digesting.

Miss Teatime said that she would like nothing better than to entertain the two visitors in her own home. Unfortunately, she lived within ecclesiastical precincts and had to be more than normally circumspect. They would be welcome, however, in her office in Saint Anne's Gate.

Charles said that would be marvellous and looked as if he meant it. Looking pleased, Miss Teatime reflected, seemed to be a speciality of his: she already had ticketed him in her own mind as the Happy One.

'You must allow me to give you a lift in my car – or have you transport of your own?'

'No, we came from the town by taxi.'

'It will be something of a squeeze,' warned Miss Teatime.

Charles said no, not a bit of it, for he alone would take advantage of her kind offer. Leaper could not possibly leave his post, and Simon would be glad to keep him company. Simon liked talking about dogs. He had two of his own.

Probably Dobermann Pinschers, thought Miss Teatime. She smiled and said: 'Aaahh!'

Charles declared the sports car to be marvellously fast looking. He contrasted in vivid terms the motorist's frustrations in traffic-choked London with his unhindered and rapid progress in 'these splendid little provincial places'.

The fair wagon's unwilling retinue having finally piled to a halt at the northern end of the town bridge, they took twenty-five minutes to reach Miss Teatime's office.

Charles paid close and admiring attention to the shabby staircase, the big draughty landing and the doors that had last received a coat of paint in the year of George V's Jubilee. 'If these old walls could only talk,' he said. 'Ah, yes,' replied Miss Teatime, adding silently: But thank Christ they can't.

Before shutting and locking the door behind them, she hung a card outside that promised her return in one hour. Then she placed gloves and bag on the desk, and waved her guest to a chair beside it.

'You drink whisky, of course, Mr Charles.' It was less an invitation than a confident statement.

'What a lovely surprise. Yes, I do, on the odd occasion. And it's Charles, incidentally, not *Mister* Charles.'

'Ah, yes; the instant intimacy of the boardroom and the sports interview. But my upbringing in a rectory was rather old-fashioned, Mr Charles. I have never been persuaded that ease of social intercourse was to be secured by the bandying of christian names by complete strangers.'

'Stranger? Oh, come, that's rather hard on me, isn't it?'

Charles half stood to receive his glass. His jocular manner had subsided somewhat.

'Formality of address,' said Miss Teatime, putting a small jug of water within his reach, 'is no bad thing until each person knows exactly what the other is after and at what price.'

'I stand rebuked, Miss Teatime. I shall fight my inclination to call you Lucy. Cheers.' He took a sip of his whisky.

'Your good health, Mr Charles.' She drank; then placed between them a box of small cigars, one of which she examined critically before lighting it and inhaling the first drag with as fastidious an air of appreciation as if she held a bunch of newly picked primroses.

She said: 'Your Mr Simon – the one who looks like an unfrocked priest – will not attempt to hurt that unfortunate Mr Leaper, I trust.'

'Hurt him? Good heavens, no. Why should he?'

She made a dismissive gesture with her cigar. 'A twinge of anxiety on my part. Please disregard it. Is the whisky to your satisfaction? It is something they call a straight malt, and most wholesome, I understand.'

Charles was beginning to look strained. He drank a little more, rocked his head from side to side, pouted thoughtfully, and finally drew breath and began: 'Miss Teatime, you are a woman of the world . . .'

The sudden cascade of her laughter cut him short. 'Oh, dear, Mr Charles, I thought you would never say it!'

He frowned, visibly annoyed at last.

'I am so sorry,' she said. 'Never mind, the time for propositions seems to have arrived. Please unburden yourself. I promise to listen.'

Charles said coolly: 'When I described you as a woman of the world, I was not paying you an idle compliment. We do know something of your history, Miss Teatime. We are aware, for instance, that you are an old London acquaintance of our man Rothermere. Nothing more natural than his paying you a call while he was up here. Simon noticed, of course. Simon tends to mooch about a lot when he's away from home. What did rather surprise us, though, was finding you this morning. You're a bit of an R.I.P. researcher, I gather.'

'I am interested in all good works, Mr Charles, within the modest territorial limits of this pleasant little town. And when I observe one that attracts the keen attention of Europe's third biggest food corporation, I think I may be forgiven for being curious.'

A smile spread slowly over Charles's face. 'You don't know what it means, do you? R.I.P. You'd like to trick me into telling you.' There was something challenging, goading almost, in his amusement.

'The prevalent disease of abbreviation,' replied Miss Teatime with dignity, 'has been propagated by those same agencies of public befuddlement that are so diligently demolishing syntax, proliferating pseudo-scientific jargon, and evolving ever more intimidating gobbledegook for use by gangsters posing as captains of commerce. There is not anything discreditable in failing to translate one of their wretched cyphers.'

'No,' said Charles, simply, 'there isn't. But you mustn't be so censorious. I am only trying to help.'

Miss Teatime reached for the telephone. 'Will you kindly excuse me a moment; there is a matter on which I should like to set my mind at rest.'

She dialled.

'Ah, Mr Leaper . . . Yes, indeed it is. I hope you are getting along amicably with Mr Simon . . . Oh, has he? . . . Yes, I see . . . Now tell me, Mr Leaper – I am speaking of this little secret of ours – what exactly did Digger say the code letters R.I.P. stood for?' She smiled. 'No, not Rest in Peace – I did realise that much . . . Imperial? . . . Ah, *imperilled*, yes . . . Of course, but how clever!' She listened a while longer, and nodded. 'You are absolutely right – not a word to the Fuzz, naturally . . . And chow to you, Mr Leaper.'

She put down the phone and met Charles's inquiring stare.

'So far as he is concerned,' she explained, 'R.I.P. means "Rescue Imperilled Pets". His late companions must have persuaded him to believe that he was helping them to abduct and preserve stray animals that otherwise would have been destroyed.'

'You think, do you, that he was deceived in believing that?'

'I know he was.'

'Why?'

'Because, whatever else the initials R.I.P. may represent, they most certainly have no reference to rescuing anything. The P stands not for Pets but for Protein. As you, Mr Charles, are well aware.'

'And what about the R and the I?'

'I shall work them out in time. I love puzzles.'

Charles took some moments off for thought. When he spoke again, it was with the air of having made an important decision.

'I am going to be more frank with you,' he said, 'than your knowledge warrants. Partly because you have the intelligence to fill the gaps for yourself quite quickly. Partly because I don't want you to suppose Cultox has anything to hide. What has happened here in Flaxborough boils down to this – a bit of disloyalty – a bit of trouble-making. Nothing more, believe me. So here's your lecture.

'P for Protein, you say. And you're right. P for Protein it is. And protein is an essential ingredient of animal feeding stuff. You do realise, I suppose, the absolutely fantastic scale of production of pet food in this country?'

'We are a kindly people, Mr Charles.'

He inclined his head. 'And Cultox is glad of it. The supply problem exists, certainly, but the market is very profitable. Sufficiently profitable, it might be argued, to justify unorthodox methods. Which brings us, Miss Teatime' – Charles regarded his glass, turning it this way and that – 'to the rather unpleasant core of this otherwise enjoyable dialogue of ours . . .'

He paused.

'Oh, dear,' she said.

'Which is,' said Charles at once, 'the idea you've got into your head that there has been a conspiracy to include the flesh of domestic animals in the output of our Flaxborough plant.'

Miss Teatime stared at him. 'I have suggested nothing so dreadful.'

'Only because you are clever enough to make everything sound suspicious without actually laying down an accusation.'

'You do me an injustice.'

'In that case, allow me to make amends by satisfying your curiosity.' He leaned back in his chair. 'What would you like to know first?'

She considered. 'Very well. Let us start, as a test of good faith, with R.I.P., shall we?'

'Re-cycled Indigenous Protein.'

The answer had come pat, like a delivery from a coin machine. Miss Teatime's 'Good gracious me!' followed only after several seconds of incredulous silence.

'Neatly put?' prompted Charles.

'Clever,' she conceded. 'In a jargony sort of way.'

'But shocking?'

'Certainly. In context, quite abominable. Who thought it up? Not that chairman of yours, surely? The longest word Sir Malcolm ever mastered was money.'

'I hate to have to admit this, but it isn't a Cultox phrase at all. It was invented by Parish-Biggs.' He looked up. 'You've heard of *them*, I presume?'

Millers, seaweed processors, prefabricators of discothèques, publishers, manufacturers of soft drinks, tape cassettes, disinfectants and art prints. Miss Teatime had heard of Parish-Biggs.

'PB are diversifying into pet foods,' said Charles. 'They've taken over LIK from Californian Cement, and now they're after WOOF, but they naturally would like to reduce share prices first. A really damaging scandal could shave perhaps a million off Doggigrub's market value.'

In response to Miss Teatime's glance of inquiry, Charles handed her his glass. She poured, very steadily. He was silent while he watched the slow rise of the almost colourless spirit – it was the palest greeny-gold – then went on with his story.

'About a year ago, PB were recruiting a new batch of technical staff when they came across a young woman graduate whose home was in Flaxborough. They decided she was good material for their espionage division, gave her a few months' training, and told her to plant herself in that dogs' home place as a part-time helper – what do they call it? – kennel maid. Bobby Lintz was her name. Short for Roberta presumably. Her father's a journalist.'

'He is the editor of the *Flaxborough Citizen*.'

'There's glory for you,' said Charles, it seemed almost automatically. The remark interested Miss Teatime. It indicated, she thought, a degree of reversion to type, brought on by stress. Here was a man more sophisticated, more sardonic, than he cared to be thought. Was he, and not silent Simon, the dangerous one?

'Anyway,' he said, 'she soon enlisted a helper. Apparently she has a very persuasive way with the opposite sex, if you see what I mean . . .'

The coyness jarred. It was a quickly calculated attempt to make up for the flip retort of the moment before. 'In our regional vernacular,' she informed him earnestly, 'Miss Lintz has been described as a bit warm in the arse.'

He grinned and went on. 'Her recruit, as you'll have guessed already, was a tearaway called Tring, and the reason she picked him, of course, was the fact that he was working at Doggigrub. He was also able to borrow a small truck from one of his brothers, and that was important, too.

'Before long, these two conned the Warden of the dog's home into joining what the poor fellow thought was some sort of Scarlet Pimpernel operation. That must have been easy enough: Leaper's none too bright a lad, by the look of him.

'They began dog-lifting. All were strays that nobody had claimed in the first week. The girl picked them and Leaper took them to a shed on its own. Then Tring collected a batch every now and again, after dark, and turned them loose forty or fifty miles away.'

'If I may interrupt for a moment . . .'

'But of course.'

'I appreciate this wealth of confidential information, but I am a perverse creature, Mr Charles. I keep wondering how it came into *your* possession in the first place.'

He smiled. 'Perfectly simple. One of the conspirators turned Queen's evidence. Or Cultox's evidence, if you prefer. We were being kept in the picture right up to last week.'

'Until the demise of Mr Tring?'

'You could say that, yes.'

'Tring was not your informer, though?'

'Oh, no.'

Miss Teatime nodded. 'Very well. Please go on. The story is most fascinating.'

Charles took several slow sips of whisky, then continued.

'The early part of the exercise had one main object – to build Leaper into a convinced and therefore credible witness to the fact that animals were being regularly carted away. He didn't know where; all he did know was that they went, and that they'd been marked off as "R.I.P." His own interpretation of that, you've already found out for yourself. It only adds to the picture of Leaper as the perfect dupe, ignorant of the wicked goings-on at the pet food factory across the fields.' He looked at her expectantly. 'You see what a clever build-up it was, don't you?'

'I do, indeed.'

'The final stage of the plan was this. A dog was to be picked for the take-away treatment that wasn't a stray – one that was identifiable and had an owner who'd likely create hell when it disappeared. Something easily recognisable – a bit of the beast's collar, or, better still, one of those metal name-and-address discs – was to be hacked about by Tring to make it look as if it had gone through machinery and then sent anonymously to the dog's owner – supposedly by a conscience-stricken employee at the Doggigrub factory.'

'How thankful you must be,' said Miss Teatime, 'that so fiendish a plot was thwarted before it could come to fruition.'

Charles rubbed his chin. 'Yes . . .'

'You sound doubtful.'

'We are a little anxious still.'

'I do not see why. The villain of the piece is no longer on the stage.'

He shook his head. 'The villain of the piece, as you put it is, and always was, *off*-stage, Miss Teatime. Parish-Biggs.'

'But how can they hope to gain their object now? Of their two agents, one is deceased and the other defected. I cannot grasp the reason for your continuing concern.'

Charles regarded her narrowly. 'I think you can,' he said. 'I think you extracted enough information from Leaper this morning to have a pretty good idea of what we're worrying about.'

Miss Teatime's gaze remained one of blank anxiety to understand.

Charles's patience broke.

'Bloody hell, you know damned well that the thing went off by accident while the girl was away on holiday. The idiot Leaper took it upon himself – God knows why – to pass over to Tring a dog that had actually been brought in by its owner. As a boarder, or whatever they call it. Tring promptly deported it to Yorkshire or somewhere, like the others, but he saw that this one had got an identity disc attached to its collar. He took it off, assuming that here was the job they'd been waiting for – the Big-Bother-for-Cultox job.' Charles made a gesture of exasperation. '*Now* do you see why we're worried?'

'Tring is dead,' said Miss Teatime, stubbornly.

'Certainly, he's bloody dead!' shouted Charles. 'And where does that leave us? I'll tell you. Waiting for a bomb to go off under the reputation of a multi-million pound product. And that bomb could be anywhere in England.'

Miss Teatime was frowning. 'Bomb?'

'Look . . . when the girl got back, she tried to find out from both Leaper and Tring what had been going on. Leaper told her there had been a mistake but that he'd put it right with the woman concerned. He wouldn't say any more. It seems he never liked the Lintz girl much.'

'Did she tell you this?'

'Yes, she did. Indirectly. I've never actually met her.'

'You mean, do you, that she told Harton?'

Charles nodded. 'The point is that we were left not knowing who that woman was in case she needed to be offered compensation for her loss. And what made it all a thousand times worse was a sudden awkwardness on Tring's part. Whether he'd become suspicious or not I don't know but when the girl tried to get the truth out of him he just treated it as a huge joke. He told her he'd already got rid of the identity disc. He'd put it in a very safe place, he said. In a can of WOOF on its way to the sealing machine.'

'Did she believe him?'

'No.'

'But you do?'

Charles shrugged unhappily. 'The idea has a certain horrid fascination. The packaging manager says that can could be now in any shop between Carlisle and Southampton.'

'Your bomb metaphor would seem to be all too apt, Mr Charles. I hope you will not consider it uncharitable of me to add to your troubles by making another of my idle inquiries.'

Frowning, he looked at his watch. 'Actually, I don't have all that much time, and there are a couple of things I wanted to ask you . . .'

'All I wish to know,' broke in Miss Teatime, firmly, 'is the identity of the person who gave poor Mr Tring his come-uppance.' She paused, then added: 'In your opinion, that is.'

Again, the raised shoulders. 'Odd question. Some sort of fairground accident, as far as I know. Unless you mean this talk about a woman being involved?' He waited, but she said nothing. 'All right – she's the wife of our local managing director. Embarrassing? – sure – but what else do you want me to say?'

She regarded him steadily. 'I do have some acquaintance with Julia Harton. She may have her quirks, endearing and otherwise, but homicide most certainly is not among them.'

'I wouldn't know. The police don't appear to share your view.'

'You will be wise, Mr Charles, not to underestimate the intelligence of our local constabulary. They are accustomed to dealing with far more devious individuals than the brash yokels who rank as criminals in the metropolis.'

'That remains to be seen.' He made as if to rise to his feet, but Miss Teatime held up her hand. She looked stern.

'Why did you follow me this morning?' she asked. 'Why, for that matter, did your colleague make it his business to spy upon an old friend of mine when he came to call? If you wish to enjoin silence upon me, pray do so forthwith and we shall know where we stand. I do know something about pressure, Mr Charles. I can just as readily recognise it when it is dressed as sweet reasonableness.'

He gave an awkward, cheek-puffing laugh. 'Pressure? You're really being very silly, you know. Respectable business organisations don't go round applying pressure on people. What do you think we are – the Mafia or something?'

Miss Teatime nodded. 'Very well.' She selected a fresh cigar and regarded it thoughtfully. 'If you and your friend are as innocent in matters of persuasion as you contend, I must tell you how it is done. Listen carefully, Mr Charles. Unless' – she struck a match – 'you dismantle at once whatever fabricated evidence has been assembled to suggest Julia Harton's guilt of killing Robert Tring . . .' Unhurriedly, she lit her cigar and inhaled. '. . . I shall personally ensure that there will be instituted without further delay precisely that series of scandalous events that Tring's removal was designed to forestall.'

Quite suddenly, her visitor underwent a striking change. The jollity drained completely away; the rosiness of his complexion was empurpled by the eruption of a fine vein pattern; the mouth hardened and was very pale.

'Namely?' The voice was different, too. Thin, cold.

'Namely,' pursued Miss Teatime, 'the discovery in a tin of your firm's dog food of a very un-nutritious metal disc; its reporting to the local health authority by the outraged purchaser; and the subsequent tracing of the owner of a dog that disappeared in August while being boarded at the Four Foot Haven; and finally . . . Ah, now what to end up with? A public inquiry? It could scarcely be avoided.'

She smiled sweetly, leaning back in her chair. 'And how is that for pressure, Mr Charles?'

'Stop calling me that, woman! My name is Blore, for Christ's sake. Colonel Blore.'

'Ah, a military man. Splendid. You doubtless will take a straightforward tactical view of my proposal. After you have consulted general headquarters, of course. May I then expect your reply by tomorrow?'

He stood. 'I probably shall ring you in the morning.' He bent to look at the telephone dial, then wrote the number on a piece of paper.

Without further comment, he strode to the door and opened it.

'Oh, Colonel Blore . . .'

He halted, but did not turn.

'One small addendum. The Eastern Counties Charities Alliance confidently expects a token contribution from the

Cultox Corporation. One thousand, I think, would be a nice gesture. Made out to cash.'

Blore made no move.

She added: 'The cheque would not be presented, naturally, until after Mrs Harton had been cleared of suspicion and delivery made to you of that little disc you are so anxious to possess.'

The door closed very quietly.

'No one is all bad,' reflected Miss Teatime.

Chapter Nineteen

INTO FLAXBOROUGH POLICE HEADQUARTERS TWO DAYS later walked a Mr Simon Bollinger, wholesale trading representative, of Wimbledon, London. He asked if he might see the officer in charge of inquiries into a fairground accident the previous Saturday – no, not that Saturday, the Saturday before – yes, September 6th, that would be it.

Because Inspector Purbright had gone out in hopes that a talk to the nephew of the former owner of the *Flaxborough Citizen* might settle a certain nagging curiosity concerning the disposal of the contents of his uncle's cellar, Sergeant Love was sent for.

Not even the open-countenanced friendliness of the very youthful-looking sergeant could put Mr Bollinger entirely at his ease. He confessed at the outset that he wasn't at all sure whether he had done right to come.

The sergeant thought, oh dear, it was one of *those* interviews, was it, and he said Mr Bollinger wasn't to worry: that's what the police were paid to do and would he like a cup of tea?

'About this accident ...' said Mr Bollinger, having shaken his head to the tea suggestion.

'Yes, sir?'

'I read when I was home at the weekend that you wanted to ask a lady called Mrs Julia Harton some questions about it.'

'We did, that's right.'

'Does that mean you think she was with the young man who was killed?'

Love thought, who's asking the blessed questions, me or him, and he said, well that was a possibility but inquiries were still being made.

'Yes, well, you see when I read that piece in the paper I knew at once that somebody had got things wrong and the more I thought about it the more I was worried in case an innocent person might get blamed.'

'Blamed for what, sir?'

'For the accident. If that's what it was, I mean. Things don't get put in that way in papers as a rule if it's just an accident, do they? And my wife said when she saw it, hello, there's something funny there. Of course, she knew I'd been doing calls in the area, so naturally it caught her eye.'

'Yes, I suppose it would.'

Simon's nervousness seemed on the increase. He leaned forward. 'My name wouldn't get mentioned in court, would it, if I were just to leave you with a bit of information and then go away? I don't want to be a witness, or anything.'

Love said that everything would depend on the nature of the information. If it was important as evidence, Mr Bollinger might be asked to give testimony at the inquest.

'The point is,' Simon said, unhappily, 'my wife is going to think – well, God knows what she *will* think if she gets to know what I was doing that night.'

The sergeant sought to adopt an expression at once sympathetic and encouraging. He succeeded only in looking brazenly curious.

'You see, I'd picked up this girl – well, not picked up, I don't mean anything like that, but she was just someone to talk to, and we were having a look round the fair.'

'And what girl would that have been?' Love inquired.

The question seemed to surprise Mr Bollinger, who shrugged and said he'd no idea – just a girl in the fair; he hadn't even asked her name. They'd had a cup of coffee together and shared a ride, that's all. 'It was on the Moon Shot thing,' added Mr Bollinger. 'Otherwise I wouldn't be here now. It was when we were on it that the accident happened.'

'You saw the accident, sir?'

'No, I can't say I did. I was too concerned with trying not to be sick and hoping it would soon stop. But when it *did* stop I could see there was some excitement going on, and then there was something else that I noticed very particularly.'

Simon paused. He frowned. 'I'm not telling this very well, am I? The trouble is, I didn't say anything to the wife, and now if she gets to know, she'll think I'm all kinds of a fool, taking rides on roundabouts in the middle of the night, but when you're away from home, it's different – you get fed up with four walls.'

The sergeant, who was beginning to find the disapproving presence of Mrs Bollinger rather hard to bear, was about to try and get the account back on its rails when Purbright came in.

Love made introductions and gave the inspector a précis of what the caller had said so far. It sounded woefully little.

Purbright smiled upon Mr Bollinger in a most friendly fashion and said: 'Now, sir – what was it that you noticed very particularly when you had finished flying round our Market Place?'

'I'll have to go back a bit first, actually,' said Simon, speaking with increased care, as if prizes for answers had gone up in value with the arrival of an inquisitor of higher rank. 'This coffee I told the sergeant about – we were drinking it, this girl and me, in a little bar that was still open . . .'

'The Venetian,' gourmet Love murmured for Purbright's benefit.

'. . . and opposite us at the same table was a fellow and a girl

183

wearing those motorbike get-ups – you know, leather jackets and crash helmets. And I noticed them specially because of their names. It was the queer coincidence, I suppose. You see, he kept calling her Bobby, and she called him Robert. You see what I mean? It was like the same name for both of them.'

Purbright nodded. 'Yes, sir, I can see that that would be memorable.'

'All of us at that table got up at the same time and went out into the fair. I'd promised the girl I was with to go on one of the rides, and that Moon thing was nearest, so we went up the steps and I paid and when it stopped we got into a car, or rocket, or whatever it's called, and I saw the other two – the ones in leather jackets we'd sat opposite – I saw these two get into the car behind. They both got in, I'm absolutely certain about that, and they shut the door after them, and the attendant checked it as he had the others.

'Anyway, when the ride was finished – and it wasn't any too soon for me, I can tell you . . .'

Purbright raised one hand slightly. 'Excuse me, sir, but I should like to know if you could see anything of what was happening in the car behind you. There was quite a lot of light, I understand. Did you happen to look back?'

'I'm afraid I didn't. As I told the sergeant here, I just sat tight and waited for it to come down. Then we got out and the girl went off on her own. Just said goodnight and left – no, when I come to think of it, she didn't even say goodnight. That's neither here nor there, though. What matters is what I noticed about the other pair, the two behind us.'

'Robert and Bobby.'

'That's right. I was watching when their door opened. The girl came out straight away. She jumped down and was off into the crowd before you could say knife. I thought, funny, and I waited for him to come out, but he didn't and I looked right inside and he wasn't there.'

'Are you quite sure, Mr Bollinger, that you couldn't have missed him? That you didn't have your view interrupted by all the people who were milling about?'

'No, not a chance. I didn't have my eyes off that car for a second from when its door started to open.'

Purbright looked satisfied. He went on: 'I should be obliged if you would attempt to give me a description of this girl you say was called Bobby.'

Simon stared earnestly at the opposite wall. 'Good-looking – decidedly good-looking – very dark hair. Not a tall girl but strong – she gave that impression – strong. Very feminine, though, nothing mannish about her. The hair was curly, by the way – I don't think I told you that. Eyes brown. Oh, and she was well-spoken. That I thought a bit queer – I mean, her boy friend was a right cowboy, yet *she* sounded like she'd been to college.'

Purbright allowed a little silence to round off Simon's recital. Then he said: 'You've been most helpful, sir. If you'll allow us to trespass on your time a little longer, Sergeant Love will put what you have said into the form of a statement for your signature.'

Mr Bollinger's look of apprehension was upon him once more. 'Oh, I don't think I ought to put anything . . .'

'What is the name of your firm, sir?' the inspector suddenly asked.

The question had not been expected. Simon thought quickly and produced the name of one of the more innocuous Cultox subsidiaries.

'Fleming and Colt,' he said.

'Of where, sir?'

'Ipswich.'

Sergeant Love's eager knowledgeability could not be confined. 'The Fairy Bluebell cake mix people,' he informed the inspector, proudly.

Purbright regarded the sallow features of Fairy Bluebell's

representative among mortals. 'You're familiar with Flaxborough, are you, sir?'

No, he could not say that he was. This was his first visit under a new appointment.

'A lengthy visit, though, sir. You were here on the 6th; today is the 17th.'

'It's standard practice to use Flaxborough as a base for the Eastern England area. I move about a lot. Even back home to London sometimes.'

'Ah, yes – the discussion with your wife about the accident. By the way, you'll give the sergeant your Wimbledon address and telephone number, won't you. Also your car number might conceivably be useful; a small point, but we may as well have it, sir.'

'Car? What car?'

The inspector looked concerned. 'But you do have a car for your job, surely, sir. Mobility must be very important.'

'I travel by train and taxi.'

Purbright nodded. 'Much more comfortable. You're very wise.' He turned to go.

At the door, he said: 'On second thoughts, Mr Love, I don't see that we need burden Sergeant Malley with this gentleman's statement at the moment. The inquest will have to be adjourned again, anyway.'

Bollinger glanced anxiously from one to the other. 'That doesn't mean I've come all this way for nothing, does it? It's that woman I'm concerned about, the one the papers said you were after. From what I've told you, it must be quite obvious she had nothing to do with this business.'

There was a pause. Bollinger looked uncomfortable. 'I only wanted to help prevent a mistake being made.'

'Mr Bollinger, are you acquainted with Mrs Julia Harton?'

'No, of course not. Why should I be?'

The inspector smiled. 'No, it would be a long shot, wouldn't it, Wimbledon to Flaxborough? Don't worry, sir; we shall make full use of what you've told us. Thank you for coming forward.'

When he had gone, Mr Bollinger ventured the opinion that Mr Purbright seemed rather a decent chap, and Love said yes, but he was sometimes a bit too soft for his own good, whereupon the security man from Cultox reflected that if the sergeant believed that, he still had much to learn about his superior officer.

Chapter Twenty

THE ARREST TOOK PLACE VERY QUIETLY ON THE AFTERnoon of Friday, September 19th, at the defendant's home. Neighbours were given no inkling of drama. Three people arrived by motor-car, gained admittance in a polite but casual manner, and departed, augmented by one, a few minutes later in a style no less friendly and informal. Anyone fortuitously on the watch would have concluded that here was a party embarking on a holiday weekend, for strapped to the suitcase carried from the house by one of the callers was a tennis racquet.

The brief proceedings at the special court convened in the magistrates' retiring room were similarly undramatic. Councillor Mrs Bella Purdy, JP, who had been requisitioned for the occasion from the counter of her husband's flower and garden furniture shop in Hooper Rise, listened with enormous gravity to the charge, to Purbright's evidence of arrest, and to his application for a remand in custody for medical reports. 'That will be granted,' announced Mrs Purdy, doing her best to sound as if the decision had been worked out by herself.

When the accused, whose habit of staring at Purbright with a sort of hungry devotion surprised the magistrate considerably, had been gently marshalled away, Mrs Purdy pronounced the affair 'very sad'. She was privately hopeful that the inspector would divulge what lay behind the sensational-sounding charge, but he merely thanked her courteously for her attendance and returned her to the care of the patrolman who had been waiting to take her back to the shop.

There, Mr Purdy became the first member of the general public to learn that pretty Bobby-May Lintz, of Queen's Road, had been put away and would soon be tried on the charge that she 'did unlawfully endanger life by the administration of a drug or drugs; and that further she did unlawfully cause the death of Robert Digby Tring by the administration of the said drug or drugs in a moving vehicle, namely, part of an apparatus known as "Moon Shot", in a public place, namely, Market Place, Flaxborough, contrary to the Queen's Peace.'

After the hearing, the chief constable held in his office what Sergeant Love would have termed a de-briefing session, but what Mr Chubb, less familiar with the terminology of dynamism, described simply as 'clearing up a few points about this very regrettable business'.

It was attended by Purbright and his detective sergeant and by Bill Malley, the coroner's officer.

Malley set things off by squinting into the bowl of his short, black pipe and commenting that it was just as well that cases of that kind had never come to light in The Old Man's Time. 'Hated women, did poor old Albert. Lawyers do, mostly. Wonder why.'

'Mrs Harton will be relieved,' said the chief constable to Purbright.

'She will indeed, sir. She was in a singularly unpleasant position at one time.'

'Partly through her own fault, Mr Purbright.'

The inspector conceded that Julia Harton had behaved foolishly. 'But not more so,' he added, 'than a great number of people who allow themselves to be impressed by the claims of advertisers.' She had been lucky, of course; the seemingly damning evidence of the photograph of her with an unscarred Tring might never have been proved a fake had not Grandma Tring mentioned Digger's 'poor little good eye'.

'Have we had any success in tracing this so-called Rothermere person?' asked Mr Chubb.

'No, sir. Harton persists in denying that he ever had anything to do with him.'

'Which makes Harton as big a liar as his dad used to be,' put in Malley.

The chief constable looked pained at this slighting reference to a member of the medical profession, albeit one who had deserted to California, a place where, he understood, doctors had "offices" and handled money between operations.

'There's no point, I suppose,' said Mr Chubb to Purbright, 'in taking the Harton business further? Not that I have any sympathy for the fellow, you understand; he did try his damnedest to make his wife seem a criminal. But so did she, you say?'

'Oh, yes, sir. She's been perfectly frank about it. Always with the provision, though, that she wanted no more than to frighten him into giving her reasonable divorce terms.'

'Sauce for the goose, sauce for the gander – something of that about it, by the look of things,' said Mr Chubb, looking not at Purbright, whose appreciation of homely aphorisms he had reason not to trust, but at Sergeant Love. Love obliged with a great nodding of concurrence.

'Did the girl's father have no idea of what had been going on?' asked the chief constable.

'None whatever, sir,' Purbright replied. 'Harton was a regular visitor to the house, but only as a fellow tennis enthusiast, so far as the parents were aware. Not that her intention to be the second Mrs Harton would have met with their disapproval. They have a highly developed sense of class.'

'It was she who set her cap at him, was it – not the other way round?'

'She took the initiative, certainly: she is that kind of girl. We don't know, but the probability is that she also made all the running at the start of her affair with Tring. The difference between their social backgrounds might well have slowed him up in the first place.'

'Not for long,' put in Malley. 'Not the Trings. She'll have been put to the bull inside a week, take it from me.'

'I wouldn't argue that point,' said the inspector, 'but what is quite clear now is the girl's readiness to discard a lover who had become socially embarrassing. That Hell's Angel gear was a good enough disguise for the odd jaunt – and doubtless exciting sexually, as you'll appreciate, sir – but it wasn't going to get her far with the Tennis Club set.'

'That girl was educated at a convent,' said Mr Chubb, as if deploring the modern unreliability of brand names.

'For which,' Purbright informed him, 'her great uncle made specific provision in his will. Did you know that, sir?'

'Old Marcus Gwill?'

'Yes. Apparently he considered his nephew's family unlikely ever to acquire polish from George Lintz.'

Sergeant Love had been following the conversation with cheerful, sparrow-like attention. 'Do you suppose,' he now put in, 'that he left them his fancy whisky with the same idea?'

Purbright said he doubted if any man – Gwill least of all – would carry altruism so far as that. It would have been to no avail, anyway: the half-dozen whole bottles and three or four quarterns of Glenmurren had stood neglected at the back of a shelf in Gladys Lintz's larder until the moment when they caught the eye of Bobby-May, on the forage for some palatable solvent of 'Karmz' tablets.

'You make it sound,' said Malley, 'as if she admits all this – doping the fellow, I mean.'

'It surprised me, as well,' said Purbright. 'But in fact her case isn't all that bad. She's obviously thought it out with some care. And they've managed to get Plant-Huntleigh for the defence.'

The chief constable regarded his inspector anxiously. 'I don't wish to seem to be questioning your methods, Mr Purbright, but confidences between prisoners and investigating officers always worry me a little. Confessions are not dependable, you know. Very unwise to rely on them.'

'How very true,' declared Purbright. 'Had it not been for your clear recall of Gwill's taste in spirits, I doubt if we could have moved Miss Lintz from the strong position of blank denial that she adopted at first.'

'And what does she say now?'

'She will rely, I think, on one of the oldest and most respectable defences in the world. The defence of her honour.'

The chief constable, Love and the coroner's officer all stared, but only Malley offered comment. 'Bloody hell,' he said, then gave a resolute suck at his empty pipe.

'She claims,' Purbright resumed, 'that her great anxiety was that if ever she were to allow herself to be alone with Tring, he would be unable to restrain what she called the physical side of his nature.'

The implications were too much for Love, who rather vulgarly exclaimed: 'What, in a rocket!'

'I, too, was sceptical,' said Purbright, addressing Mr Chubb, 'but she quoted as precedent his having boasted a capability of being intimate (again, her expression, sir) with a motor-cycle passenger whilst actually riding the machine. This did tend to haunt the latter days of their relationship, according to her, and she took precautions accordingly. Hence the tablets, which a married acquaintance had assured her would have a temporarily emasculating effect upon any intending seducer.'

The chief constable considered, thin lips compressed, mild eyes directed at a point in mid-distance beyond the dusty window pane. 'Just credible, perhaps,' he conceded. 'But a pretty weird tale, Mr Purbright. I shall be very interested to see if she gets away with it.'

Malley addressed Purbright. 'What did you make of that

commercial traveller fellow who popped up at the last minute?
Bollinger.'

'The mystery witness,' supplied Love, zestfully.

The inspector answered only after a pause. 'I didn't believe
him.'

Mr Chubb looked alarmed. 'Would you mind explaining
that, Mr Purbright? As I understood the matter, this man
Bollinger's testimony was the first and only piece of direct
evidence that Tring and the girl went into that thing together.'

'Oh, I believe *that*, sir. They were together. The girl doesn't
deny it. Whether Bollinger watched them as he says' – Purbright shrugged lightly – 'is something else.'

'You do not suggest, I hope, that we are putting up a
witness who will be discredited by the defence?'

'Oh, no. I'm sure he knows what he is doing. That is what
I found disconcerting, as a matter of fact. There is a carefully
concealed professionalism about the man. He made only one
mistake, and that was a fairly trivial one. He had Tring
addressing the girl as Bobby.'

'A perfectly natural abbreviation of Roberta.'

'Quite so, sir. But it so happens that her close friends invariably call her neither Roberta nor Bobby, but Bobo.'

The chief constable winced and murmured 'Good Lord'.
A moment later, he added: 'Very easy to mis-hear with all that
fairground row going on.'

'Very, sir. But what Bollinger claims to have done is *over*hear.
And that I should have thought absolutely impossible in the
circumstances.'

Mr Chubb consulted his watch. 'Well, gentlemen, if there is
nothing else you wish to ask me . . .' He allowed a count of
five, then began to assemble hat, gloves and stick. 'Time and
Tide,' he said, with a smirk of wry amiability, 'to say nothing
of the Corporation Traffic Committee, wait for no man.'

The others prepared to depart.